Inspiration

To order additional copies, please contact us.
BookSurge, LLC
www.booksurge.com
1-866-308-6235
orders@booksurge.com

RACHEAL DAVID

INSPIRATION
Tainted Love

Name of Publisher
2006

This series is dedicated to my darling husband, my forbearing mother, my three lovely children and to all injured nurses around the world.

Inspiration

Racheal David is the pen name of a powerful new writer. Born in 1951 David spent long periods of her childhood in the hospital, and vowed to give something back. She became a State Registered Nurse in General Nursing, Public Health Care, Midwifery and Mental Health care, until a fall forced her to quit working. Not one to give up, she embarked on her new career as a writer. She lives with her forbearing mother, her loving husband, and their three gorgeous sons in Hemel Hempstead in the United Kingdom.

CHAPTER ONE
Child Prodigy

It was six o'clock in the evening. Papa Addo was relaxing in his hammock under the mango trees in the cool evening breeze, after the day's hard work on his cassava farm. He was puffing up at his fired clay tobacco pipe. Mama Addo was getting ready to go to the regular Friday social evening of cultural drumming, dancing, games and story telling. Every villager looked forward to this Friday evening events as they worked extremely hard on their farms during the week. The events were held in the large open place, next to the market.

Papa and mama Addo have been married for five years. Unfortunately, mama Addo had not been able to hold down a pregnancy to full term. She had lost five pregnancies before five months. She was expecting triplets in her third pregnancy but she miscarried. Mama Addo was devastated. She consulted priests and medicine men but she went on to lose the fourth and the fifth pregnancies as well. Rumors went around that an aunt of mama Addo, Naa Baley, was an evil witch and that she ate the baby's hearts whilst in the womb.

Papa and mama Addo were so distraught that, they decided to give up trying for a child. Some villagers strongly believed the anecdote that mama Addo was losing her pregnancies because of the evil activities of her witch aunt, Naa Baley. The myth was strengthened by the fact that Naa Baley did not have a child of her own. Mama Addo had an elder sister called

Mama Terley, affectionately called "Maa T". Mama Terley did not need a proof of this myth even if one existed. She believed it wholeheartedly.

It was common knowledge that childhood injuries last long. Maa T never saw eye to eye with Naa Barley when the former was a teenager. Naa Barley never saw anything good in Maa T. She would always find fault with Maa T, no matter what she did. Naa Barley would go to the extent of manufacturing false stories about Maa T and telling such to people when Maa T was not around. In almost every case Maa T was not guilty of whatever she was alleged to have done. In the few instances when Naa Barley appeared to be correct, the story was an overwhelming exaggeration.

The story of the evil witch, gave Maa T the opportunity to get her own back at her aunt. One Friday morning, Maa T gathered a few friends who also believed the myth that Naa Barley was a witch and was preventing Mama Addo carrying pregnancy to a successful end. Maa T and her henchmen paraded to the market place, where Naa Barley was selling peppers and tomatoes. Numbers increased as the troop went along, some joining without knowing for what reason. It was as if they were going to war. To Maa T it was more than a world war. They were armed with clapping sticks, tambourines, pans, bowls and drums. The market place was populated and boisterous that morning. People in the market wondered what these "warriors" were up to. When they got into the market, they started hooting, shaking violently the tambourines, clapping the sticks, beating the drums and the metal bowls discordantly. They chanted and shouted Naa Barley's name, hurling insults at her for chewing the hearts of Mama Addo's babies in her womb. It was a spectacle to behold. Maa T paced with valor to Naa Barley's stall and started addressing her.

"Look at me. I am voluminous. I have more flesh on me to chew than the tiny babies in my sister's belly. You can have me and leave my poor sister alone."

The clapping, the drumming and the shouting grew wilder as if they were "possessed" by the gods of Oboboshibie. It did not bother Maa T a bit whether the allegation about Naa Barley was true or not. Maa T was contented that she had carved her revenge at last. Naa Barley appeared surprised and shocked at what was happening but never uttered a word. The party left Naa Barley and danced round the village, singing and drumming.

Papa and mama Addo had absolutely no hint of what Maa T and her friends were doing that morning. They had gone to the farm.

Unknown to Maa T, Mama Addo was into the third month of her sixth pregnancy when she and her friends confronted Naa Barley. Six months later Mama Addo gave birth to a bouncy baby girl. She was born on a lovely spring morning in the West African village of Oboboshibie. Her birth brought joy to both the maternal and paternal sides of the family. On the seventh day after the birth, the traditional "outdooring" and naming ceremony took place. She was held up to the gods by an older relative with acceptable character and the usual incantations said.

"To you our fathers I present our new arrival. May she have favor with you."

With washed hands she dipped her finger into a calabash of the non-alcoholic corn wine and touched the baby's lips three times. Saying,

"May you know the difference between water and alcohol."

After this short ceremony, Ama was returned to her mother in the room. The outdooring continued.

A chosen older man with good reputation chaired the ceremony, and poured the libation asking the blessing of the gods for the baby. This is held early in the morning.

Chairman: Agoo
Gathering: Amee.
The above was repeated three times.
Chairman: Twa, twa, omanye aba
Gathering: Yao
Chairman: Jee wogbee kome
Gathering: Yao
Chairman: Wobolekutu wokpe
Gathering: Yao
Chairman: Woje bu. Woje nu.
Woye wonu wokoji ano ajo wo.
Yao
Gbo ni ba nee, esee tuu, ehie fann
Yao
Oba nine kome wohele bo niji enyo.
Yao
Oyi aba gbo jen
Yao
Wekumeiabii ana faanii afa o
Yao
Ga Humi le Kooyoo twaa dani ewieo
Yao
Ona onako
Yao
Onu onuko
Yao
Oyi ana wala

INSPIRATION

Yao
Oke edin ba oke eyen aaya
Yao
Ke otsu nii le kaimo otse ke onye.
Yao
Twa omanye aba
Yao

Every line of the incantation was followed by tipping a little of the corn wine onto the ground, the last drop was tipped with the last response by the gathering.

Papa Addo presented a bottle of akpets to the chairman and said,

"The name of my daughter is Ama."

Everyone at the ceremony was given a tot of the akpets to drink in acknowledgement. Those who did not drink took a sip and called Ama's name.

She was named Ama because she was born on Saturday. Maa T gave Ama a nickname, Dromo, which means grace. Maa T always called her Ama Dromo.

The picturesque village where Ama was born sat on a hill surrounded by spectacular mountains and dense green forest. The village blended into the stunning surroundings without a trace as the houses were constructed out of mud and roofed with thatch.

Ama was the apple of her parents' eye. Her milestones were a joy to observe. She crawled at six months, took her first step at eight and by nine months was walking unaided. She was an active, boisterous child and never stopped giggling. As an only child, her parents, though uneducated, were determined to give her the best things in life they could afford. Things they were not privy to as children. In particular, they wanted their child to be educated to the highest level. Education, for them, would be the greatest gift they could ever give their child securing her future and hopefully theirs.

They spent many excitement-filled and sleepless nights discussing and dreaming about Dr Ama Addo, President Ama Addo, and Chancellor Ama Addo. In Papa and Mama Addo's dreams their child filled virtually every position of power and prestige. Education would unlock opportunities. Their child would be great, a visionary. Dreams would be realized. After all dreams did come true, did they not?

Ama started primary school at the tender age of six. The village school she attended was only a stones throw from her home. Pupils gathered under the huge Pila Pila tree for classes. The branches of the tree spread wide and provided shade and protection from the elements. Classes always proved to be fun and were interlaced with stories of village myths, music and dance. Every pupil knew of the myth of the Pila Pila tree, how its branches spread out at night to gather and haunt pupils who absconded and did not put hundred percent efforts into their studies and respect their elders. Ama did not need any encouragement or scare tactics to motivate her at school. She excelled in her studies throughout her years at primary school and received several prizes for hard work.

One day when she returned from school, she rushed to her mum, who was very busy in the kitchen preparing the family dinner.

"Hi, Mama" she said. "I think I have an idea of what I want to be in the future. I wish to be a doctor. We had a visiting health practitioner from the hospital in town and she told us about the work doctors do. I felt an immediate desire and enthusiasm. I want to be helping the sick in our community, just like the visiting health practitioner."

"This is excellent news" her mum replied. "You are very

ambitious and I admire your enthusiasm to excel. I know you will make us all proud. However, you must understand that you have a long way to go with your education before you can enter this rewarding profession. We shall discuss it when Papa returns from the farm."

Ama, still excited by the earlier school visit ran to get changed out of her school uniform and rushed back to help Mama finish the dinner. Papa arrived just in time to enjoy the family dinner. Mama who was overwhelmed with joy could not wait to break the exciting news to her husband on his return. Upon hearing the news he blurted out with joy "This is great Ama! At last, we will have a scholar in our own home. You will achieve what we have always dreamed of doing but could not because we had to go straight into work in order to help the family. We are so proud of you Ama, so proud. It is a noble profession.

" You must be conscious that the type of profession you have envisaged entails a lot of sacrifice and hard work. I have heard that sometimes doctors find it very difficult to have time for their loved ones, let alone themselves. They are so busy and very involved in looking after patients. Sometimes the stress even breaks them down and they turn to drugs and alcohol. I mean look at doctor...."

Mama Addo, on noticing where the conversation was heading, quickly intervened to ask Papa and Ama to come sit for dinner. During dinner the conversation soon came back to Ama's news. Mama Addo gave Papa a stern look of disapproval in relation to his earlier comments as he again started advising Ama. Telepathically Papa got the message and soon changed his tack.

"I shall come to your school later to discuss this with your class teacher in order to find out what we can do to help you achieve your ambition," he said in between the large morsels of food he was shovelling down his mouth.

"Thanks Papa. I love you all and appreciate your support. I will make you proud of me," Ama replied. Papa looked lovingly at his daughter and murmured, "We are already proud baby."

The next morning she left for school, Her mind wrought with her dreams of being a doctor. She found it difficult concentrating on what the teachers were saying during most of her early morning lessons. During the lunch break, and still bubbling with enthusiasm, she approached her teacher and asked, "Could you tell me how to become a doctor?"

"Oh yes, your father spoke to me about the subject and we will have further discussions later. You just keep working on those grades. We shall have our own little chat soon."

One day when Ama returned from school, she told Papa and mama Addo that they had a poetry lesson by their new poetry teacher.

"We were asked to write a poem about any subject we felt passionate about. Each poem was read in class in the afternoon. We had lots of laughter. Naa Awaa wrote a poem about the coconut tree. Her description of the coconut tree fitted that of a man. Another made us laugh a lot about a poem of the six puppies. She had observed what the puppies did each time she went home. What she had observed the puppies do was very interesting indeed. We clapped for her. She would have got the prize if the teacher had put a prize on the best original poem."

"What was your poem?" Mama Addo asked Ama invitingly.

I could not think of an original one so I wrote a poem, which I learnt at school. I think my teacher at the school wrote the poem herself as she was always writing new poems whenever she was not busy. My poem was entitled:

CONTENTMENT

. . . .

That happy state of mind, rarely possessed
In which we can say we have enough,
Is the highest attainment of Philosophy
Happiness consists not of possessing much
But being content with what you have.
He, who has little, has enough.

"That is an excellent poem," Mama Addo said. It is worth being memorized by every child to recite each morning in the class.

Papa gave a cynical laugh of appreciation that spoke a lot.

Ama was pleased that Papa and mama liked the poem.

There was unusually long silence. Suddenly Papa broke the silence. He was reflecting on a wise saying by an intelligent old man when he was young. This was at the story telling night. He told Ama the wise sayings, which Ama transcribed into a poem. She read the poem in class at the next poetry class and won a huge applause.

BE THOROUGH

. . . .

Whatsoever comes your way to do
Do it with your entire mind
Never be only a little true
Or only a little right
Trifles even lead to heaven
Trifles make the life of man
So in all things; great or small things
Be as thorough as you can.

The class teacher wrote it down in beautiful cursive letters and encouraged the whole class to learn it off by heart. The class described the exercise as "chew and pour."

Ama continued to work hard. She won a scholarship to one of the top secondary schools in the country. She maintained the habit of winning accolades for her academic achievements. It was no surprise when she graduated with the best results in the history of the institution.

Further doors opened for her as she won a scholarship to study at the Medical School of Excellence. Her hard work seemed to be paying off. What a privilege to be educated in one of the best medical institutions in West Africa. Her life was quickly becoming a rag to riches story. It was the talk of her village and made headlines in the town newspapers; "The humble beginning of a child prodigy...farmer's daughter wins scholarship to top institution."

Back in her village a durbar was being planned in her honor for thrusting the name of Oboboshibie village into the limelight. Papa and Mama Addo would be the proudest parents in the whole world.

CHAPTER TWO
Oboboshibie Village.

It was about three weeks to the end of the last term of Ama's school life in Oboboshibie and the pre season rituals for the yam festival were also about three weeks away. Life was relaxed, as there were no more exams to take or serious class work for Ama's class.

It was suggested by the civics teacher that the class were going to research Oboboshibie village and the yam festival to discuss in class. The class was divided into two groups; one group was to research "Oboboshibie Village" and the other "The Yam Festival". The teacher added that the student or group, who would produce the best dissertation, would be given an award during the impending yam festival.

The students were naturally excited as the mere mention of one's name for good work by the village chief at the ceremony carried a high honor.

Ama belonged to the group researching Oboboshibie village.

At dinner, Papa Addo reminded the family that the rituals preceding the yam festival were about three weeks away. Ama immediately recollected the assignment about Oboboshibie village and the yam festival.

"Oh yes, Papa," Ama interrupted. "You have jogged my memory. We are to research life in Oboboshibie village and the yam festival to discuss in class.

"Grandma would be the best person to consult. She loved telling stories about Oboboshibie," Mama Addo advised. " Custom, however, demands that you will have to "wash her feet" with "Akpets", our local gin. She would pour libation to ask the god's permission to tell you the story. She would then gulp down the rest of the "akpets" before commencing the story. If you fail to "wash her feet", she would not be in a position to tell you as the gods would punish her by letting her go mad."

The onus would be on her to pacify the gods by acceding to their requirements through the long ceremonial sacrament of libation and alcohol consumption.

After dinner Ama ran to buy a bottle of the village's finest "akpets" and a small gourd containing "tawa", shredded dry tobacco. Grandma would smoke the "tawa" in her ivory smoke pipe whilst narrating the story.

Grandma was very pleased to be asked by Ama for the story of Oboboshibie. At nightfall the family gathered around the naked fire. Ama had informed the cousins that grandma was going to tell the story of Oboboshibie and invited them to come along.

It was a small crowd around the naked fire as grandma poured libation. Grandma held the calabash in both hands as Ama poured the Akpets into it with the solemnity that the gods deserved. She tipped the drink on the ground and said

"Agoo",

The group responded, "Amee".

"Agoo"...........…"Amee"

"Agoo".........…"Amee".

"Fathers, your permission I seek this evening. What I forget may you remind me. May those who tell the story live, may those who hear the story live."

"*Yao*," the audience echoed in agreement

She tipped more of the drink on the ground and drank the rest at a single shot. She reached for her ivory smoke pipe and loaded it with the "tawa".

Ama helped her to light it. Grandma puffed at the pipe with an air of satisfaction and commenced to narrate the story.

"Many, many new moons ago, our ancestors lived in the village of Langote. Langote was the biggest of all the surrounding villages.

They were farmers. Each market day, which was held once a week, the products of the farms were brought to the Langote market for sale.

It was very busy on the market day, overflowing with people and foodstuff. Many traders came to barter in bulk to sell on their local markets. There was much hustling and bustling to attract customers' attention.

On one fateful market day, a fight broke out on the market between Yamte from Langote and Odrame, a young man from Draso village. They had both gone with their wives to barter foodstuffs. They saw a good bargain they were both interested in. Heaven knows what evolved a furious fight ensued. Both men were good wrestlers in their villages. Odrame was hurled upside down above Yamte's head and thrown head down on to the floor. The incident happened too quickly for anybody to intervene to separate the combatants. Odrame's head hit a small rock on the ground, splitting his skull. Odrame died instantly.

In the village of Langote, it was a taboo to kill, whether intentionally or inadvertently. The punishment for such abomination was banishment from the village of Langote. Before Yamte returned to the village, the news had spread like wild fire in the harmattan season. It was on the lips of every Langotean.

The village chief summoned Yamte. The fetish priest and the village elders were also in attendance as the custom commanded. They informed Yamte that as a result of the murder in the market place, he had offended the goddess of the earth. Custom demanded that he had to pacify the goddess with one white she-goat and one bottle of akpets. The blood of the she-goat was sprinkled round the village to pacify the gods. The following day, Yamte and his family were banished from Langote. There was wailing and gnashing of teeth by Yamte's household and friends.

Friends packed their cassava and other foodstuffs and animals for safekeeping. Later on the friends bartered some of the foodstuffs and animals left by the outlaws for cowries and expensive beads. The proceeds were to be sent to Yamte and family at a later date.

The friends helped to pack their valuables into head loads to take away.

At dawn, before the cock crowed, Yamte and his family were on their way to Oboboshibie. Yamte's three wives, twelve children and three brothers set off on their exile, beating a hasty retreat. Yamte's brothers were not obliged to go as the custom did not include siblings. The brothers could not bear to see Yamte go alone with his wives and children. They volunteered to go with their elder brother.

As soon as they left, the young men of the village burnt their huts and barns to the ground. The young men had no ill feeling against Yamte and his family. They were only carrying out their customary duties. The will of the goddess had been accomplished.

The journey to Oboboshibie was to take them five days

to complete. On the second day of their journey, they stopped to rest and have some food. They roasted cassava to eat with fish baked half dried. Whilst the women in the party were preparing the food, Yamtè's eldest son, Kuet, went into the bush to clear an area and dig small holes in the ground for the group to defecate into. Long after the food was ready, Kuet had not returned. The party got worried. Two brothers of Yamte set out to find out why Kuet was not back yet. They found him sprawled on the ground, unconscious and foaming at the mouth.

Kuet was dead. The poisonous gray snake, very common in that area, had bitten him. The party was thrown in more distress. Kuet was buried where he was found.

Yamte and his party arrived at Oboboshibie on the fifth day. On arrival, there were only five families in the village. Two of the families were close relatives. They welcomed them with open arms.

Papa Odua was the uncle of Yamtè's wife, Mama Abele. Papa Odua ordered his sons to bring two pots of palm wine and a bottle of akpets. He poured libation and they drank the palm wine. Papa Odua's wives had gone to the stream to fetch water. Papa Odua had suspected the reason of their sudden arrival at Oboboshibie because of the composition of Yamtè's party. He made a short speech welcoming them.

"It is peace here by the grace of the gods. You were on the road," an expression which up to this day invites visitors to tell the story of their journey.

Just before Yamte began to speak, Papa Odua's wives returned with pots full of water. They were invited to greet the party and left to prepare food. The tradition in our part of the world has been that anyone who enters your gates must be fed. They brought mounds of "kokonte" and peanut soup prepared with large chunks of goat meat and copious mushrooms and snail. Kokonte is powdered dry cassava stirred in boiling water, on fire, into thick paste and molded into balls, the top of the balls of kokonte was coated with okra paste tinted with palm oil. Kokonte and peanut soup have the reputation of breaking heavy sweat when eaten. It is thus nicknamed "opolatsa", the sweat-breaker.

Papa Odua insisted that they finished eating before Yamte gave the account of their mission. In the meantime, they had a long chat about their families back home. Papa Odua asked about everyone by name. He seemed to remember the names of the whole village.

It was unusual not to have eaten kokonte or fufu for five days or more. They especially enjoyed the food and they washed it down with more palm wine. Pawpaw was served as dessert.

Yamte gave a detailed account of what had brought them to Oboboshibie unannounced. Yamtey's children knew for the first time the sad incident involving their father. Papa Odua was quick to praise Yamte for his prowess. He regurgitated that Yamte had made him proud. He would have been sad if Odrame had thrown Yamte. Papa Odua had taken pride in watching Yamte wrestle when the latter was young, because Yamte was good then. As for the sad event of Odrame, Papa Odua asserted that it was a pure accident, which was not the first to happen and would not be the last. Indeed it happened to Papa Odua also many new moons ago. That was why he and his entire family ended up at Oboboshibie.

Yamte's party were given a place to sleep. At cockcrow, the next day, all the men in Yamte's party went with Papa Odua to the farm. The women were left to keep the children occupied, especially the new arrivals. On their way, Papa Odua pointed out to Yamte an expanse of his land he was going to give Yamte and his brothers to farm. When the party was returning home from the farm, Papa Odua showed them plots of land on which they could build their huts. They would, however, need to greet the village chief, offer drinks and sacrificial cockerel and officially put in a request for plots to build on.

The children had already settled in as if nothing had happened. They were playing and running around the compound in groups and pairs. The lassies opted to play "ampe". "Ampe", as you all know, is a game of wits between two players. The two players hop on both feet synchronously. Player One tries, to guess which leg her opponent puts forward suddenly when their feet touch the ground after the third hop. Player One must also put forward her adjacent leg simultaneously (right leg to left leg) to win a point. If Player One shoves forward a left leg whilst Player Two thrusts out her right leg then Player Two gets the point. The player to get to five points wins a round. It can be played at any speed depending on the agility of the players and the legs must be thrust forward on the third hop, clapping as they hop. Watching the play made the old folks to remember their youth.

That evening, Papa Odua took Yamte to see the chief of the village. He provided the customary gifts on Yamte's behalf. The chief priest, Ote, was summoned to invoke the blessing of the goddess of the earth for Yamte and family.

The chief granted the request for land to farm and to build.

As the tradition of the village was and still is, the whole village helped Yamte and families to build their huts. Soon there were four more compounds and thirty new settlers of the community. The village continued to enlarge as the numbers of compounds and inhabitants increased. The previous footpaths and narrow roads were turned into broad roads, covered with red gravel though not tarred. When the road was improved the villagers decided to plant nim trees at uniform intervals along the windy main road to the village. Grandma was proud to announce that she was actively involved in the planting of the trees.

Now the pictorial view of the arrangement of the nim trees along the main road to the village gives a false impression that one is about to enter a botanical garden. Although the modern utilities of the cities, water, electricity, and public telephone had only started trickling into the surrounding villages the houses have retained their time-tested architecture; round huts of brown mud roofed with thatch in a semicircular compound.

Each family lived on a large compound enclosed by a thick wall of brown earth, and punctuated by the round huts. A single wooden gate opens into the compound. The contours of the wall follow those of the round huts giving the compound a semicircular look. These architectural arrangements were quite unique to Oboboshibie village. Papa Addo's hut like other heads of families is the first to meet as one enters his compound. Papa Addo elected to keep only one wife and therefore sleeps in his hut with mama Addo. Ama sleeps in the second hut. Others with more than two wives had a hut for each wife. The wives shared their huts with their young children. Papa and Mama Addo were lucky to have a storage area in the kitchen. In families with many wives and children to one man, four or more children sleep in one room with bags of cassava, yams, maize, beans and other foodstuff. And of course, the famous rats."

The children's faces lightened with excitement as grandma mentioned, "rats".

"The rats emerged during the night to eat the grains when the children had not gone to bed. We heard of the occasional bites from a rascally rat, arousing the children from their deep sleep with a scream. A couple of Grandma's audience nodded their heads to testify to this amid bouts of laughter.

The children used metal traps made in the village to catch the rats. They attached fermented dry fish as baits to attract the rats. But even the rats can learn. A few rats were killed and the rest quickly learnt to avoid the fish bait. Sometimes the children poured boiling water down the rat holes. They succeeded in killing the rats but days after the rats decompose and the offensive scent could be smelt many houses away. The room could not be used for many days. Some children chose to lure the rats out and chase them with sticks to kill them. To some boys this became a sport."

Grandma paused for a gulp of the "akpets" and a few puffs at her pipe. She took pleasure in telling the story as the children enjoyed listening to it.

Grandma went on to tell them about the famous Oboboshibie rat story. Everybody accepted as true.

"Life in Oboboshibie was communal. The villagers loved to do things in common. In fact Oboboshibie was a village where everybody was another's keeper. The inhabitants would happily tell off other native's children for wrong doing and even punish them without expecting hostility from their parents. In fact, the parents would appreciate them for correcting their children. The saying goes that one woman gives birth to a child but the whole village brings her up.

Over the years the citizens of Oboboshibie contributed to accumulate large quantities of expensive jewellery, including various sizes of gold chains, expensive beads and cowries. The collection was given to a respected head of family in the village whose husband was deceased. The said head of family was grandma's great aunt, Mama Fia. The people of Oboboshibie would borrow the jewellery for important occasions such as customary rites during the yam festival or marriage ceremonies for a small fee. The fees were used to acquire more ornaments.

It was told that the time came for an occasion. Mama Fia was approached to borrow the trinkets to dress the young teenagers at their initiation into adulthood during the yam festival. The jewellery was nowhere to be found. Mama Fia went to the box in which the ornaments had been safely tucked away, all those yam festivals. To her astonishment, the trinkets had disappeared. In frenzy, Mama Fia combed the whole hut but did not find the collection. Mama Fia decided to move the box.

Lo and behold, there was a rat hole at the corner of the floor. Despondently, Mama Fia came out to announce to the families waiting to collect the ornaments, that surprisingly, she could not find the jewellery. The villagers were amazed and disappointed. They were short of telling Mama Fia that she was telling a fib, but for the deep respect inherent in the village for a family head.

They left very dejected. Some of the families even shed tears. On the way back, they gossiped amongst themselves. One wondered whether Mama Fia had sold or bartered the jewellery to settle a secret debt.

A few days before the ceremony, three village boys were playing behind Mama Fia's compound and spotted a rat hole. They inquisitively attempted to explore the hole with a stick. Before plunging the stick, one boy noticed a reflection down the hole. They resolved to explore some more. They went for hoes and started digging around the hole to enlarge it.

Whilst they were digging, Papa Akpiti, an old man of the village saw them and admonished them for digging behind Mama Fia's compound without her permission. Papa Akpiti warned them that Mama Fia would beat them up if she found out what they were doing.

The boys explained to Papa Akpiti that they found a rat hole and saw something flickering like a star in it. They were trying to find out what it was. Papa Akpiti drew nearer to look down the hole. He confirmed the boys' statement. He left.

Aware of the rumor circulating in the village regarding the lost jewellery, Papa Akpiti went inside the house to alert Mama Fia of what was happening behind her compound. The boys had dug sufficiently and were now certain there was a significant evidence of a shiny object, which needed to be brought out. One boy ran out and returned with a hooked branch of a tree. Just when the boys were about to insert the plunger, Papa Akpiti and Mama Fia arrived. They looked on whilst the boys retrieved one of the jewellery.

Thrilled, Mama Fia encouraged the boys to continue digging. Soon the whole of the jewellery set was raised to the surface. The story spread very quickly, being on the lips of every adult in the village in a matter of seconds. They trooped to the scene.

Mama Fia apologized again most sincerely for the distress they had suffered. She told the gathering that she was going to send the trinkets to the goldsmith to be polished before handling it over for the ceremony, which was only three days away.

As Mama Fia walked away, reminiscing the discovery, she felt a tinkling blow of satisfaction spreading all over her like "zomi" palm oil does on hot "puna" yam marsh.

When Mama Fia returned to her hut, she inquisitively turned the wooden box upside down and noticed a big hole at the corner of the box. The rat had chewed a hole in the corner of the box through which they had carried away their loot.

The village of Oboboshibie was located in the middle of the thick rainy forest in the eastern part of the country. The background is a mountain, which spreads on both sides embracing the village on its chest. There is a winding stream emanating from the hills many walking days up country. The stream drains into a moderate size lake at the foot of the mountain on the outskirts of Oboboshibie village. Children enjoy swimming in it at weekends and during vacation.

At dawn, the villagers set off to their farms. The women carry baskets containing their machetes and water. The young men carry a raffia sack over their shoulder containing machetes, gunpowder and their snuff gourds. The elderly men carry their guns over their shoulders and cutlass in the right hand in case of eventuality. On the way to the farm, anyone they encountered was greeted by name, as everyone knew every other by name. The birds were chirping on the odum, wawa and pilapila trees. The chirping made inviting accompanying "music" for the villagers on their way to the farms. They work hard till late morning, when they stop for breakfast. The meal often consisted of roasted cassava with roasted wild snails and mushrooms, washed down with palm wine. In the late afternoon they trek back carrying foodstuff and game they had shot.

The chief's palace has a different architecture though still of mud and roofed with thatch. The huts are rectangular and big with a huge compound, which encloses several other huts and the "gbatsu", the prophecy room of the chief priest and the traditional courtroom. The chief has as many wives as the number of compounds in Oboboshibie village. The walls are painted with yellow clay and engraved with traditional symbols depicting the position of authority. The durbar is held in the huge compound opposite the chief's palace.

The open market place has several wooden stalls; a few are roofed with woven palm leaves."

Grandma tipped the last drop of the local gin on to the ground to signify the end of the story.

The children breathed a sigh of contentment. Though it was getting late the children were not feeling sleepy and asked for more. Ama therefore asked if grandma would tell them about the Apaapretu story or the yam festival.

Grandma said that tipping of the last drop of the akpets was the sign of the end of story telling. She promised them another session the next evening.

The children agreed and dispersed.

When grandma arrived the next day, the children were already seated. The attendance had improved a little. Word had gone round that grandma was telling interesting stories. Grandma said hello to the children and sat down, She did not pour libation, as grandma did not feel it was necessary to ask permission from the gods to continue her story. However grandma took a gulp of the akpets before commencing the narrative.

"Not long ago and even to this day, villages in and around Oboboshibie, and for that matter the whole country, if not the whole of the West African sub region, worshipped their dead bodies. This was because of the deep respect or fear of the spirits. The villagers believed that the spirits of their loved ones always went to their forefathers. It was believed that the forefathers came to take the deceased spirits away the evening of their burial. It was generally held that the spirits would bless them if the villagers prepared food for the spirits, their spiritual guardians. The encouragement the villagers had was that the forefathers always ate the food left at the graveside, at least so they thought.

The procedure was to prepare foods that the deceased particularly liked. Three or four young women would carry the food to the graveside. The young women were members of the family of the deceased. The food was laid on the grave in the evening of the day of burial. In fact, the villagers left no stone unturned to prepare the best quality food for the spirit of the forefathers. It was the practice to visit the graveside at dawn the next morning, to see if the grave was still intact; whether the dead body had not been tampered with. Three female elders would be sent to inspect the grave the next morning. The ladies would report back their findings.

Some young men and women could not comprehend why the best part of the food in the family was given to a dead person, especially if they knew that the deceased was so ill that he or she could not eat for long periods before his or her death. A story was once told that a very poor beggar, called Apaapretu from Bianor village ate a food offered to the spirits of the ancestors but did not die, as everyone expected.

Three young men from Oboboshibie village wondered whether they would also live if they tried it. They did not need convincing. They decided to try it. Okri, one of the three adventurous young men suggested that to accomplish this feat they would need to get themselves very intoxicated. One Friday afternoon, the three daring men heard that somebody had died in Bianor village. The funeral had been planned for that Friday afternoon. They went to the drinking bar to lay foundation with akpets. They got the drink on credit, promising to settle the account the next day. Then they invited themselves to the funeral. They took active part in the funeral obsequies and they accompanied the funeral parade to the cemetery for the burial. On their return, the rascals went back to the bar for reinforcement. They knew there would be palm wine to go with the food that would be brought to the graveside so they were careful not to get themselves stone drunk. They played draughts to while away time. Soon it was approaching the delivery time. They started drifting towards the cemetery. The gang found a suitable place to lay ambush. Without fail, Okri and his friends saw four not-too-beautiful young women carrying earthenware of the servings and pots of palm wine to the graveyard. When the rascals saw the women, they exploded with joy. They were careful not to attract the attention of the women. The women placed their loads on the grave, said a few invocations and left.

As soon as the women were out of view, the rascals surfaced. They were quick on the mark. They set off to work on the acquisition. The food was not only well prepared but warm too, let alone the pot of the frothing good friend, the fresh palm wine. The men devastated the food specially made for the spirits of the dead. They thoroughly enjoyed the food, watering it down with the pot of fresh palm wine sitting next to the food. The gang enjoyed the food so well because they were not related to the deceased. The food that evening was maize meal ("banku"), accompanied by okra stew, containing pig feet, snails, mushroom and quality smoked fish. They returned to Oboboshibie very drunk, swaying and swerving like a battered boat on a stormy sea.

At dawn the next day, as custom dictated, three elderly women from the family of the dead visited the graveyard for the inspection and to lay flowers on the mound. Before they got to the cemetery, one of the old ladies broke down in tears. Spontaneously, the others responded with a chorus of tears. When they got to the grave, the earthenware had been wiped clean and the pot of palm wine had disappeared.

"The forefathers had visited," one of the women, said, the

tears drying from her eyes. They laid the flowers on the grave with the usual incantations. They chanted thanks and praises of the forefathers. They left to report their findings.

Meanwhile, at Oboboshibie, Okri and his friends were waiting to see the repercussion of their deed; whether they would die. There was no reaction. Okata, one of the three young men even joked that he slept very well and he opened his bowel especially smoothly the next morning.

The day following their visit to the graveside, Okri went to Bianor village to monitor any gossips regarding the food they had eaten the previous day. He saw a young woman coming out of the house of the deceased. Okri started conversation with the woman. Okri learnt that the family of the departed was glad the forefathers had visited. It had been suggested that another round of the food would be sent to the grave that evening. She was on her way to the market to purchase ingredients for the food. Okri chuckled.

Okri returned to Oboboshibie. On his way back, he saw Brikiti chatting with his sister.

"Hei, Brikiti, come, come,"Okri beckoned to his ally in crime.

"*Egbee shi ekonn.* It is round two today. I am just from Bianor village. The people are going to send another ration of food to the graveside today." Okri reported with a good smile.

At four the three musketeers set off to the grave again. As anticipated, the food had arrived. The meal consisted of big balls of yam fufu served in earthenware and steamy hot chicken palm soup. They pounced on it demolishing the mountain of fufu and the palm wine.

Three young teenagers had gone to the bush near the cemetery to hunt for birds with their catapult. They heard crackling of dry leaves as if someone was walking towards them. They went into hiding. Soon the boys heard talking and laughing from the direction of the cemetery. They decided to investigate. One of the boys was an able climber. He was soon scaling a tree nearby. From the tree, he noticed three men eating on the grave. He recognized Okri and Brikiti. He climbed down quietly. They decided not to disturb them.

The next day the story was around the market place. The story found its way to Bianor.

Ama asked grandma what happened when the story got to Bianor.

Grandma heaved a sigh and told the children that it would be rest day the next day and discussion on the Yam Festival the following day.

CHAPTER THREE
Yam Festival

Grandma, tonight is when we are meeting for the story of the yam festival," Ama reminded grandma.

The audience was seated well before the appointed time for the meeting. The children were buzzing with excitement because of what yam festival meant to them. Two of the children had not been to any of grandma's story telling sessions before. They brought grandma two small gourds full of dry shredded tobacco. The old lady was full of praise for these young intelligent boys.

"Is this a bribe?" grandma joked.

"Oh no grandma, we all love you and we want to show our appreciation for the good stories you have been telling the younger ones," said one of the boys, who saw the humor.

"We could not attend the story telling grandma but we heard all that you told our brothers and sisters. I belong to the group in school researching the Yam Festival. We want to win the prize so that our group would be mentioned at the durbar next week."

"Hei, Shoga, so that is a bribe? I will tell my team mates that you have given a bribe for the best narrative on the Yam Festival," Ama declared under tongue.

Those in the audience who understood the meaning of the local expression "talking under tongue" broke out in exhilarating laughter. Toga, one of the children told grandma that the expression "talking under tongue" was coined by one of their classmates and it meant, "mumbling". She put it in her poem."

"Don't be harsh on the poor boy, Ama," grandma joined in the fun.

"As you are aware, Oboboshibie and the surrounding villages are at the end of the fifth week of the rituals that preceded the yam festival. It was the "peace" period. The villagers were in festive mood.

The rituals begin with the town criers going to bang the drums round the villages to announce the beginning of the Yam Festival. The Chief Priest and his hierarchy of priests and priestesses conduct a short ceremony at the gates of the chief's palace depicting the planting period. The priests are all dressed in white robes with white hats made from calico with frills all over it. They carry brooms to signify cleanliness. They wave it around driving away the spiritual filth of the previous year. The rest of the ceremony is done in strict confidentiality, at night. It is supposed to be the secret of the goddess of the earth. After this ritual, the priests parade in single file to the outskirts of the village and using new hoes, simulate the clearing and preparation of the land for planting of the new crop. They clear a small area, dig out and plant the new seed. All of these are preceded by the pouring of libation, calling on the gods for plentiful rain and good harvest. After this the chief priest announces that the "Peace Period" has officially commenced. During the five weeks following, the chief priest decreed that no one in Oboboshibie and its adjoining villages were permitted to beat drums, clap, shout or make any form of loud noise. It was a taboo to die during the peace period. Any member of the royal family who died during the peace period is not buried until after the ban had been lifted. The chief priest and his subordinates have responsibility for the funeral ceremonies of the royalty and the peace period is a holy period for them. They were not supposed to touch dead bodies. That is why the royalties were not buried till after the ban had been lifted. Also, a chief cannot be buried without drumming and firing of guns. Ordinary villagers who died during the period were allowed to be buried but under strict observance of the "no noise rule".

During the peace period, individuals and villages at loggerheads were to find reconciliation. Everybody is under obligation to foster peace in his or her settings and between villages.

The Yam Festival is the occasion for giving thanks to the goddess of the earth and honoring the ancestral spirits. The festival must be celebrated before anyone else tasted the new yam. The gods had to partake of the new yam first. It is the annual event of great expectation. The yam festival celebration is the time when many villagers, living outside the confines of the villages come home. The population swells up significantly. The villagers look forward to seeing their loved ones, who have been away working, trading, marrying and even the few university students. The children especially are full of hope that their uncles and aunties would grace the occasion with their presence and thereby spoil them with gifts and sweets.

The ban on this year's peace period was lifted last week and the whole of this week as you have observed already has been the week when those living outside have been coming in. Many of you have already been to the outskirts of the village to welcome the parties. They come in their decorated trucks and buses and the passengers are dressed uniformly in traditional clothes. One can feed his or her eyes with the variety of designs and patterns. They sing and drum and dance all the way from wherever they have come from. Some villagers go to the outskirts of the villages to welcome them and join in the merry making, drumming and dancing all the way into the villages. Drinks never stop flowing during this week and the next."

Grandma paused and placed a goatskin bag she had brought on her lap. The children looked on eagerly expecting grandma to pull out her pipe. But out of the bag came large quantities of sweets. The children marveled. Grandma asked Ama to help distribute the sweets to the children. A member of the audience shouted amusingly,

"Grandma is this a bribe?"

Shoga replied for grandma.

"Grandmas never give bribes. They give gifts so that the children would listen to their stories attentively."

The children as well as grandma laughed.

Ama interceded on behalf of grandma informing the children that her (Ama's) auntie brought the sweets from the city and since grandma is very generous, she always shared what she had.

Grandma lighted her pipe, took a few puffs and continued the story. But before grandma resumed the story, Shoga pointed to the pipe and said,

"Grandma is enjoying her sweet, the soothing smoke."

"There will be wrestling tomorrow, Friday and Games on Saturday," grandma continued. "The mobile cinema van has never failed to come and show us a film on the Saturday after the Games and before the main events of the Yam Festival, which come off the following week. We have seen the same film for the past two years. I hope it is something different this year. The young men of Oboboshibie will pitch their strength in wrestling against the might of their counterparts from the adjoining villages. It is always exciting evening. There is intervillage "ampe" duels between the young girls of the various villages. The older women vie for the accolade in "oware", not forgetting the older men at the draught competition. The young who feel able are permitted to enter the draught competition in the young men's category. You will remember that Papa Addo won the coveted crown in draught last year. The respective winners would be mentioned at the durbar next week.

The Yam Festival week begins next Monday with the celebration of the "Agbaa" deity. It marks the cooking of the new yam and the partaking of it by the Agbaa deity. The celebration opens the way for anybody to eat the new yam. Female members of the village help to cook the meal on the forecourt of the chief's palace near the "gbatsu", the prophecy room. Large quantities of the new yam and eggs are boiled and the yam mashed. The mashed yam is mixed with palm oil. The hard-boiled eggs are peeled and served with the mashed yam. Before the inhabitants taste the mashed yam, the gods have to be fed first. Then the chief priest, accompanied by his subordinates, pour libation to thank the gods for taking care of the people of Oboboshibie and its neighbors. They go round the villages sprinkling the mashed yam and crushed eggs, everywhere. This is done early in the morning. When the gods have tasted the new yam the door is open for everybody to eat the new yam. Large numbers of goats and fowls are slaughtered and a big meal is prepared. This is commonly yam fufu with goat soup. Chicken stew is also made to go with yam porridge. It is a mighty feast and everybody is fully fed, both visitors and villagers. Everybody is welcome to partake of the feast. Pots and pots of palm wine are drunk, let alone the local akpets. The merry making continues well into the night.

The festival of the twins follows the Agbaa deity festival on the second day of the new yam festival. It is believed that the twins have special powers bestowed on them by the twin goddess of Blema. Special rituals are therefore performed for them. This ritual is always performed on Tuesday. It was alleged that the goddess of the twins ordered that Tuesday must be set apart for the twin celebration each year. Some of the neighboring villages celebrate their twin festival on Friday. It has been difficult to find a suitable explanation for this discrepancy. The people just believed it was the will of the gods. The gods are consulted each year for what the twins want to be done for them. It is believed that when the parents offer the twins what the gods have asked for the twins the parents would receive blessings from the gods. On the morning of the Tuesday set aside for the twin celebration, the chief priest and his assistants formulate a concoction in a large wooden bowl. Apart from leaves, which are obvious, nobody, except the chief priest knows what the composition of the mixture is. The twins and their parents bath with the concoction. It is compulsory that the twins bath with the potion. The immediate family members however oblige. It is believed that the formulation strengthens the twins and purifies others. Women, who want children and notably twins, are most likely to bear twins if they bath with the fabrication. At least, that was the belief. Fresh mashed yam with palm oil and hard-boiled egg is prepared for them. They eat with their friends and families. In the afternoon, the remnants of the concoction are carried to the bush to throw away. Only volunteers are allowed to carry the wooden bowl containing the relics. Anybody is allowed to volunteer to carry the load to the bush to dispose of usually near a stream. The twins are dressed uniformly, usually in white but not mandatory. It is interesting to note that as soon as the bowl is placed on the head, the carriers are "possessed" by the spirits of the gods of the twins. They move uncontrollably and talk

monosyllabically. No action or utterance is under the carriers'
will power. There had been several occasions when people had
disbelieved and challenged this. Two years ago, the wrestling
champion openly challenged this assertion. He averse that it
was fictitious for the carriers to claim they had no insight into
what they were doing or saying. That it was a lie for the carriers
to maintain that a spirit possessed them just by placing the
bowl on their heads. His best friend had experienced this and
had confirmed that it was true. They took a secret bet. Last
year the young wrestler agreed to test his disputation. On the
day of the Twin celebration, this energetic wrestler, volunteered
to carry the bowl of the concoction. The time came for the
bowl to be heaved on to the volunteer's head. He stood there
in pensive mood. It would be interesting to know what he was
thinking about at that very moment. The crowd was especially
thick this time because of the rumor circulating about the
"Doubting Thomas". Two males, who had twins themselves,
lifted the bowl, containing the remnants of the potion, on
to the head of this healthy, young wrestler. No sooner had
the bowl touched this young man's head than he was off on
a hundred meter dash still carrying the bowl. He raced all
over the place, uncontrollably. A portion of the crowd heard
him to say the god of the twins were asking that the twins
be dressed in "batakari", the gorgeous princely Enugu attire.
The gods did not release their grip on him until he tipped
the contents of the wooden bowl. Then he regained his self-
consciousness. Instead of the crowd booing at him, they rather
clapped for him. What was curious about this was that he had
absolutely no recollection of the event. He disappeared with his
head between his thighs. Hopefully he will never challenge the
provisions of the gods again," grandma observed.

"The rituals of initiation into adulthood would then

follow the rituals of the twins. Some of you have gone through this phase already. You will be able to tell your friends what happened to you," grandma suggested.

Bronya raised her hand and offered to tell them what was done.

"There were thirteen of us, six boys and seven girls. The boys were on one compound and the girls on another. An elderly man took charge of the boys and a respected elderly woman was the head of the team that looked after us. We were confined in two rooms for three days. We ate, slept and received lectures. We did not know who did the cooking. We had lectures on how to comport ourselves in public and in personal hygiene because we would soon start visiting "the back of the houses" (the local expression for menstruation). I do not know what the boys were taught," Bronya paused for a response from the boys. None came so she carried on.

"We had long lectures on the danger of misbehaving with boys or with men in general. We could be pregnant if we messed around with men. We were taught how to avoid temptations on this front. We were to have children when and only when we were ready for it. The gods bless children who keep themselves well in their youth. The elders looked after us in association with three priests of the village. They had secretly thrown the sacred "twadis" to find out which of us were not virgins. A concoction was brought from the prophecy room to our compound and I believe the boys also had one. We were to bath with it. Virgins are the only people allowed to bath with this potion. It is a curse to lie to the gods if you know you are not a virgin. We were warned of the consequences, which included barrenness, and round the board failure in life. The chief priest came to visit us and to inform us of who had been found by the throwing of the twadis, to have lied to the gods. It was anxious moment. The chief priest was happy to announce that the gods were pleased with all of us and that the oracle had showered their blessings on all of us. That meant the priests found during the throwing of the "twadis" that we were all virgins. Indeed we all knew we had not had unhealthy association with men before. We bathed with the concoction with confidence. I am expecting Kaple to tell us how many of the boys were caught out for indecent behavior. On the morning of the third day we were served with the delicious "ofotro", the celebration meal. The fourth day was the out dooring. As everybody knows we were gorgeously dressed and heavily decorated. Pillows were tied around our waist to increase our girth. We had generally gained a lot of weight from the overindulgence with the food during our confinement. The Kente cloth was wrapped around us from just above the breasts to the toe and tied above the waist with a strong woven cloth. The shoulders and the upper part of the chest, not covered, were oiled and beautifully painted with white clay mixed with the sweet scented juice from that plant in the bush. We were already pretty girls but we were beautified even more with the communal jewellery, elegant cowries and garland. Our traditional hair-do decorated with gold studs won many hearts. The gold anklets had tiny bells attached to them and they made sweet sounds when we moved. We then danced in front of the large gathering in the grounds near the marketplace.

Oh, I forgot to tell you that we were also taught the correct way to do the traditional "odoye" dance. We all agreed it was the most enjoyable day of our lives. We had loads of gifts.

But above all we were now "women" commanding all the respects of the older folk," she concluded, with pride.

None of the boys volunteered to speak so grandma declared the meeting closed.

"The final day of the Yam festival is the durbar, which is due in a couple of days. I give you all my best wishes at your discussions in school tomorrow." grandma gave the closing statement.

The meeting closed with a chorus of "thank you" from the children to grandma. A few of the girls gave grandma a hug.

The discussions on Oboboshibie village and the Yam Festival by Ama's class is scheduled for today. The pupil of the school had been advised to report to school at ten in the morning instead of the usual eight o'clock. The pupils had absolutely no idea how big the head teacher and her staff had planned the occasion. When Ama's class teacher informed the head teacher of what the class had planned to do, she decided it would be nice to invite the Chief of Oboboshibie and his henchmen and some elders in the village to attend since it was the penultimate day of the Yam Festival. Ama was very astonished to see, on arrival in school, that the chairs had been arranged as if for prize giving day. The astonishment of the students was compounded by the arrival of the village chief with his entourage and other invited guests. Many more uninvited guests showed themselves in occupying the seats for the pupils. Many of the students had to stand. They were happy to stand. The head teacher introduced the prominent personalities and the guests and told them the reason of the unusual gathering.

"Today is the last day of our final year students," she said. The students, in consultation with their able teacher came up with this plan to discuss the Oboboshibie village and the Yam Festival. There are two groups; one group will discuss Oboboshibie village and the other group will talk about the

Yam Festival. It is about two weeks now since they have been researching the topics. I am sure they have worked very hard at it. My colleagues have kindly requested the Chief to be the sole judge and to tell us which group has made the best presentation. It was a "mouth-watering" and very informative discussion. The students had extrapolated grandma's stories and added so many interesting points, which grandma was surprised to learn. The pupils and guests showed their appreciation with a long round of applause.

When they finished the head teacher thanked the speakers and all contributors for the excellent exposition. She also thanked Ama's class teacher for his vision. The head teacher then invited the chief for his verdict. The chief often spoke through his linguist. After a long deliberation, the linguist got up to relay what message the chief had given to him.

"The chief expresses his profound gratitude for the school's invitation," the linguist said and commented at length on the contents of the discussion. He said the chief has been aware that the school teaches our children well and the school never shirks its responsibility to educate the children on the sacred traditions of our forefathers. The linguist commended the teaching staff for their dedicated work. The linguist never stops talking unless he is poked. He went on and on until the children started to fidget. Their patience was running out. They wanted to hear the winner of the discussion.

"I hear what you say, children," the linguist said. "The chief has asked me to say that the talks were so informative and so amusing that he has found it difficult to pick a winner at this time. He says he would go and sleep over it and see whether he would be able to pick a winner."

The children were disappointed because they wanted to know which team or person was going to be mentioned at the durbar the next day.

The head teacher declared the meeting closed and officially announced the end of the school term. She wished the final year students all the best in whatever they found themselves doing.

The day of the durbar was greeted with a shower of rain. The villagers had prayed that the gods gave them a clear dry day. By nine in the morning however the rain had stopped and the thick gray cloud overhanging Oboboshibie, appeared to be moving away. The villagers breathed a sigh of relief. The children were soon out jumping and running around, singing;

Rain, rain, and go away,
Go and come another day
Oboboshibie children have a durbar.

After Papa Addo and family had had their fill of fufu and okra soup for lunch, they set off to the durbar ground. Ama was feeling nervous for what was going to happen to her at the durbar. The village was already buzzing with people in various gear and dresses. It was more than a fashion show. Sounds of the traditional drums had filled the air inviting the villagers and all to the durbar. The drums speak. The most interesting part is that on this occasion the young men of the village play the drums. It has become a tradition for boys who have been initiated into adulthood to learn to play the drums. Drums sit around on the palace compound and everybody is invited to go and learn how to play the drums. The young sons of the village deem it a pride to learn how to play and there are elders there at all time to teach the young folk.

The durbar ground was packed full. The young men of the various villages were holding their hands as they defined the inner confines of the durbar ground. They had no problem keeping the spectators outside the inner circle. The chiefs of the adjoining villages arrived in their palanquins carried on the shoulders by strong men. The chief's "kara" sat in front of him in the palanquin. The "kara" is a six-year-old boy believed to be the "soul" of the chief. Queens have girls as their "kara". Their entourage followed the chiefs, the drummers hammering the drums with the specially carved sticks. Others played the flutes made from tusks of large animals, including elephants. People were dancing to the tunes of the drums. Others danced to meet the parties from the adjoining villages and danced with them to the durbar ground. The numbers continually kept swelling. The chiefs from the neighboring villages got seated.

The unmistakable tune of the durbar sounded. It announced the arrival of the Oboboshibie Chief. He was gorgeously clad in Kente cloth and decorated with gold ornaments. He was carried in his beautifully decorated palanquin, his "kara", sitting in front of him. On hearing the sound of the drums, the whole crowd exploded with joy, clapping, dancing and waving scarf and handkerchiefs. Some women spread their over clothe on the ground for the chief to walk on them, signifying their respect for their ruler. A path opened gracefully in the crowd like the parting sea in the "Old Testament". The big drums following the chief to the parade ground suddenly became silent as if heaven had opened to swallow them.

The presence of the Oboboshibie chief was greeted with more gunshots. Some had reserved their last gun powders for this point in the celebration. The hunter's guild always gave a display, as the chief was about to enter the inner circle. Their uniform was a spectacle to behold. On the arrival of the chief they dashed around the inner circle, shooting their guns into the air. They banged the shaft of their guns against each other's, and threw the guns in the air. The gunshots saw the little children scampering to their mothers for protection. The air was not covered with dust as it had rained in the morning. The hunters then left the center of the circle.

The official drummers for the durbar, already seated, started playing their various sizes and shapes of their drums and flutes and the other entire accompaniment. The chief stepped forward with poise, wearing gorgeous kente cloth and gold chains and donning his head with a magnificent gold crown. He acknowledged deafening cheers with his ever-present "ahurudja", which is alleged he uses to fan away evil designs thrown at him by the wicked. He wore native sandals made out of hide and decorated with gold and kente cloth. He took short calculated footsteps, wriggling his upper torso in a graceful harmony to the gesticulations with his hands. He was holding the sword of power, the staff, in his left hand and the "ahurudja" (the "swat") in his right. The audience understood his motions. He inched towards the drummers and touched the drum in the front row with the staff. The drumming stopped abruptly as the staff made contact with the drum. The mass gave a standing ovation. The chief was helped to his seat.

The loquacious linguist waited a little for the chief to catch his breath then he got up to introduce the chiefs of the villages, beginning with the chief of Oboboshibie, who incidentally was the senior chief. Had something unusual not happened, the linguist would have protracted with his speech.

A truck suddenly pulled up at the durbar. A group of energetic men in smashing regalia scrambled off the truck. They carried miniature paddles and a minuscule canoe. They were apparently of the fishing stock. Only the inhabitants of the coastal cities and towns had the privilege of seeing fishermen in such stunning regalia. They had their own band, which set to work as soon as they set down. They went places with their "Kpanlogo" music and dance. They won tremendous applause.

Soon the whole crowd was in to the "kpanlogo" dancing. The "abele" variety was captivating. The chiefs were so impressed that their leader was permitted to address the gathering.

"Thank you for your warm reception. We got the exact response that we had anticipated. A good man from this part of the country lives and works in the capital. His name is Lawyer Alpomah. He and his wife frequent the beach to buy fresh fish. He spoke to me about this wonderful celebration here and asked if we could come as his guest to this durbar. He did not need to wait for days for the answer. We told him straight away that we would come. He could not come with us but he sent us with Papa Atreku, whom you all know. We are happy to be here." Papa Atreku was invited to the front and everybody clapped for him. The chief gave a message to the linguist to deliver openly to the fishermen's guild. It was an open invitation to the fishermen to come to the palace after the durbar.

For once, overwhelmed by all that had happened, the chief decided to break tradition and address the gathering. The linguist and the elders would not be part of any breach of tradition so they did not allow him. The chief whispered something into the linguist's ear.

"Honorable chiefs, fellow villagers, we have come to the main item of our gathering when citizens who have excelled are mentioned," the linguist went on.

Ama's heart started to race.

"Your majesty has asked me to tell you this."

He gave a long pause as if to count Ama's heartbeat.

"He said, yesterday he was invited to adjudicate upon a discussion in our school. The decision was difficult to arrive at yesterday so he came home to sleep over it. I am now glad to announce the chief's selection of the winner."

"The group that discussed.........................
The.................Yam Festival."

There was pandemonium. The winning team ran to the center of the circle jumping, shouting and hugging each other. They then went forward for the congratulatory handshake from the chief. Even Ama laughed and clapped.

The village-dancing troupe consisting mainly of children below the age of twelve years gave a display of the various dances of the villages. It was nice to watch.

"Now," the linguist went on, "this year the various competitions were very well contested. Atakonko of Mokoee village won the wrestling match."

Atakonko acknowledged the claps as he stepped forward for the congratulatory handshake.

"Papa Addo successfully defended the draught crown and Mama Foka won the "oware" competition," the linguist concluded. The winners went for their laudatory handshake. Ama smiled broadly as her father went for the handshake. She was as proud of him as she knew Papa Addo was proud of her.

The linguist called the head teacher of Oboboshibie School to come forward. She walked with head held high, and an air of fulfillment to the linguist. She was asked to read the citation for Ama. She did not have a script. She recounted the academic achievements of the young woman not forgetting her agility at the high jump. The comment on her high jumping drew further applause.

Ama was called forward and she received a small token of a book and the head teacher placed a garland over Ama's neck. Ama got the congratulatory handshake from all the chiefs and even from the loquacious linguist.

Papa and Mama Addo were the proudest parents that day.

The head teacher invited the captain of the school (the senior prefect) to come forward for congratulatory handshake for good all round work in and for the school.

As it was the tradition, all the winners, including the fishermen's guild retired for the chief's palace for refreshment.

They were watered and fed to bursting.

CHAPTER FOUR
Uncharted Waters

Once all the hype and excitement surrounding Ama's move to the city to commence her medical studies had subsided, Papa Addo sat her down to bring home the reality of the journey she was about to take. He enjoyed imparting his wisdom during their frequent father-daughter talks.

"Ama!" Papa Addo called, "listen and listen good," he emphasized "You are about to enter a world completely different from the sheltered life you are used to and within which you have been brought up. Life out there is poles apart from ours. You will be independent and will now have to make decisions on your own. We won't be there to pick up the pieces all the time.

"With freedom comes great responsibility. And with responsibility comes temptation. You will have to keep your wits about you, and maintain the values we have instilled in you. Do not be afraid of anyone or anything but be courageous, and in any stressful situation seek help. Go with our blessings and may the gods of our ancestors protect and direct you in all your undertakings."

Though her parents were proud to send her away, it broke their hearts to see their only daughter leaving. It seemed like it was only yesterday when she took her first steps unaided. They watched once again helpless as Ama took another step towards fulfilling her dreams. With each step she tasted the fruits of freedom and was open to choice. Her parents were well aware of the pitfalls of freewill and in particular the temptations of the city. Their only hope was the belief in the discipline and values with which they had nurtured their daughter. Ama felt her parents' concern and sadness. She reassured them that she would make them proud and keep in continual touch.

The big day came and she finally left home for a new life in what were 'uncharted waters.'

She arrived on campus with a burning desire to succeed. Like the other first year students, it was very early when Ama arrived on campus. After the admission formalities were completed, all the first year students were advised to meet in the auditorium. It was normal practice for one of the fourth year students to welcome the first year students, give them a brief history of the school and to show them around the various departments.

"Welcome to the school. Four years ago I was in the same position as you. My name is Margaret Amutu. The medical school, as you know, is our dear country's first school of medicine. It is a faculty of the nation's first university. It is a modern institution commissioned by Parliamentary Instrument initiated by our very ambitious first chief minister after the country gained independence from her colonial masters.

It was opened in the late fifties. Stories have it that the architecture was fashioned on a leading medical school in Europe. No wonder, therefore that it has all the amenities and departments that any leading university would have.

Once the client is willing to pay for the service, whatever details of the architectural drawings the client requests would be included. The chief minister was so thrilled about the prospect of a modern medical school that he was prepared to meet any cost for a modern drawing. He got just that!

The construction of the school progressed satisfactorily during the first couple of years. Then the money allocated to the project ran out. Rumors were flying about that a good portion of the designated money had found its way through some individual's leaking pockets into foreign bank accounts. They were rumors all right, but how many of those were true?

The heated exchanges in the country's parliament gave credence to these rumors. It was, however, the chief minister's resolve that the medical school should be opened on schedule. He would not allow any unfounded rumors to derail his ambitious project. This however led to short cuts. A senior administrator of a government department, with no expertise in design and civil engineering, plunged his pen on to the architectural drawings of the school and crossed out those parts of the drawing he believed were not important, in order to cut cost. This led to some of the completed buildings without some important provisions. For example, some of the mounted automatic hand dryers were chucked off, some wards did not have sluice rooms, and the number of offices and outpatient rooms were reduced. Unfortunately the senior administrator had a heart condition, which required surgery and he had had his appendix removed. He had also had operation on his hemorrhoids the previous year. As one would expect this senior administrator did not cancel any of the drawings of the surgical department," Margaret paused as the class burst out in uncontrollable laughter.

All these shortfalls were rectified much later with a large government subvention.

The entire teaching staffs of the medical school, during its inception, were made up of indigenous doctors and specialists.

They had no experience of running a medical school but they were inspired by the chief minister to get on with it. They turned out a brilliant set of doctors from the school comparable to any newly qualified doctors anywhere in the world.

We will, hereby, resolve never to be the exception," Margaret said with her right hand on her left breast.

The whole class rose in unison shouting vows of approval with hands on their chests.

Margaret continued, "The pediatric department has a hostel for mothers to come and stay in whilst their children are on admission. Indeed for mothers who live far away from the hospital. The radiography department has modern facilities, including ultrasound, C.T Scanners and magnetic resonance imaging (MRI) machines. There is facility for radiotherapy in the main theatre, which has twenty-four Theatre Rooms on three floors. Theatres on level three are used solely for cardiac operations. In addition to the main laboratories, each clinical department has their own "mini laboratory".

The medical school is about half a kilometer from the main hospital compound. There are ten lecture theatres; four here in the medical school and the remainder in the main hospital. The Nurses Training College is next door, Margaret said cynically. The boys smiled mechanically. The large laboratory services with its training school are at the north end of the hospital as is the pathology department with its big mortuary. As the adage goes, one cannot blow a whistle on an empty stomach, I will show you the canteen, let alone the library and the pharmacy.

You would have realized by your constitution that the medical school now admits students from far and wide." Margaret concluded amid hearty clapping from the class. " Less I forget," Margaret shouted at the top of her voice. The clapping drowned her shouts. She continued to shout, now gesticulating violently. The shout died down.

"For those of you interested in sports, the hospital doctors have a Tennis Club in the hospital. They have asked me to extend their warmest invitation to anyone who wants to join them. They play twice a week- Tuesdays and Fridays from five thirty in the evening. They play on the two courts behind the maternity hospital." Margaret was interrupted by a large yell from the back of the auditorium

"Subscription fees?" Kojo demanded.

"You students are "unbiz", no money —so you do not need to pay dues. Those of you whose parents are rich can contribute and those of you who are poor can donate according to the strength of your arms. They appear to enjoy themselves playing the tennis. Each Friday evening after the tennis, they meet at the canteen for refreshment. They organize tournaments with other Tennis Clubs in the city," Margaret ended.

Four senior students divided the class into four groups of twenty-seven each and they were taken on tour of the hospital.

After the familiarization tour, Ama proceeded to the warden at Dedei Hall. She was assigned room number 24, which was on the ground floor. The hostel was a three-storey building, the blocks fashioned like a maze. After unpacking she made herself comfortable on the bed.

Ama reminisced her journey to the medical school. She reflected on how magnificent the hostel was. She had read in the university brochure that the hostel was built in the late fifties. She looked to see if she could find rat holes at the corners of the room. Ama wondered whether there were rats in the city. She knew that a house in Oboboshibie would not stand for thirty years without one or two rat-holes appearing.

Consumed in her reflections, she fell asleep.

It was six o'clock the following morning when her roommate awakened her. Her roommate had just arrived and Adzo was also going through the formalities of unpacking and becoming familiar with the room.

"Oh hello," Ama mumbled as she awoke from her slumber, her eyelids still heavy from the night's sleep. Her new roommate turned out to be a second year medical student called Adzo. She didn't seem interested in staying around to chat with Ama and left the room as quickly as she had come in. Ama found that initial encounter a bit untoward. It wouldn't have hurt Adzo to, at least, extend her a nice welcome especially as she did disturb Ama's sleep.

Adzo is light-skinned and short, barely 1.2 meters tall. She has a pair of perfectly formed breasts, like fruity melons, and commands large round melting eyes. Her nose is well proportioned with neatly cut lips. She is cute.

Adzo hails from the capital. She attended a mixed high school. Adzo was made to skip a class because her intellect and academic performances were far above her age group.

In the results of the first Bachelor of Medicine (1st M.B.) exams recently released, Adzo had obtained distinction in physiology and biochemistry. The lecturers anticipated that Adzo would clear the board in the second Bachelor of Medicine exams (2nd M.B.).

Ama had formed the impression that Adzo was bumptious.

Aba, another first year student, knocked on the door and entered the room as Adzo walked out.

"Hi I have just moved in next door. I have no roommate yet. Do you mind if I joined you? I overheard your brief conversation with your roomy. She seemed a bit rude."

" I have also formed the same opinion, please sit down. She aroused me from my sleep, I said hello to her and she ignored me," Ama agreed. Aba and Ama hit it off immediately and the conversation flowed without much effort. Aba, being the extrovert of the two led the conversation.

"She may be thinking we first year students are nonentities; not deserving her attention or company. Maybe that was what happened to her when she was in her first year, and therefore wants to maintain the "tradition". Remember what happened to greenhorns in the high schools. I had a rough time as a greenhorn in my first year in Ketebreka. I thought this practice would never happen in universities," Aba wondered.

"I suppose this practice of initiation of greenhorns happens in boarding schools only. Some boys in our school attempted to introduce it but the headmaster of our school outlawed it immediately" Ama reiterated.

"This is sheer nonsense," Ama thought.

Aba felt compelled to narrate the myth of Ketebreka

"Ketebreka School sits on a hill surrounded by extensive green field which is punctuated by huge mahogany and pila pila trees. The school is a hundred and seventeen years old. It was constructed with stones excavated from the Ketebreka hill and roofed with colorful slates, which were locally made out of clay and sand fired in a very hot oven. The windows and doors were carved from wood felled from the forest. The school has gone through extensive reconstruction. It was said that during the construction of the school, many of the workers lost their lives or sustained serious injuries. The families of the victims were awarded bursaries to attend the school. One recipient of such a bursary, Mrs. Afiyeye, excelled academically and became the headmistress of the school. Some of the houses were named after the victims.

Mrs. Afiyeye, popularly known to the students as "Afiee" played important part in putting Ketebreka on the academic map and has since remained one of the top high schools in the country.

"In Ketebreka," Aba continued, the first year students were called "homos" during the first week of the first academic term. It was the initiation period.

It was a wet September afternoon when my mum and dad drove me down to the school. In the presence of my parents the senior students of my house, Okropong House, were very warm and cordial. They carried my metal trunk, containing my clothes and my wooden "chop box", to my bedside in the dormitory and even helped me make my bed. My mum left no stone unturned to ensure that I would not be in need of anything. My "chop box" was full to the brim with, at least, two dozens of sardines, both powdered and evaporated milk, sugar, chocolate powder, gari and three bottles of top quality "Joebed" black pepper (chilli sauce) and other provisions.

Our parents had to leave as the bell rang summoning the whole school to dinner. In the dining hall, the Senior Prefect (captain of the school) welcomed the first year students and wished us an enjoyable academic year. She said our parents had gone to a great length and endeavor to bring us here. Education is the best investment any parent would make and hence advised us that we should not waste this golden opportunity.

The dinner was "Jollof" rice accompanied by chicken curry stew. Desert was banana fritters and custard. I was so nervous that I could barely eat half of my ration. The classes were mixed in the dining hall. There were thirteen students on each long dining table, six students on either side of the table with one final year student at the head of each table. The student population was eight hundred and fifty.

After dinner the whole of the first years were asked to stay behind to meet with the final year class. At the meeting, the entertainment prefect nicknamed "Chimbo" addressed the class. Chimbo was also the fifteen hundred meter champion of the school. At inter-school sports meets she would invariably be the last. Then the roar of chimbo would rise and fill the air like smoke emanating from a volcano.

Chimbo, chimbo, chimbo...The tired and weary chimbo would always respond to the cheers and would sprint to the finish, albeit still last. Chimbo was always looking to entertain the crowd.

She told us that for the first week of this term our title would be "homo". When we were asked our names we would say " homo" before mentioning our actual names.

"What is your name?" chimbo pointed quickly at me.

I responded rather pompously, "Aba Danto"

All the final year students glanced at me, a couple of them started to shuffle towards me. It was a scary moment.

"Hei ninny, how dare you! Did you not hear what I have been saying the whole evening?" chimbo snapped.

"And you what is your name?" directing her left second finger briskly at Josdain Banku.

"Er.... r...r Homo Josdain Banku" "homo" Josdain Banku she stuttered.

"Exactly," chimbo teasingly replied.

Aba picked up where she left off.

"There is a myth of Ketebreka, which had been told for a century. It is about a ghost in the school. The ghost comes wandering in the dormitory at night, visiting the bedside of the "homos"."

At the mention of ghost, I immediately felt an irresistible urge to empty my bladder. I must go otherwise there would be an accident. I rushed out of the room to return ten minutes later. My re-entry was greeted with mumbling at the back of the room. Those at the front of the room wore a stern, rather enquiring facies. I expected a reprimand from chimbo but none came. Chimbo had not said a word since I scurried out of the room.

Chimbo recapitulated the myth story on my return.

"I was saying that there had been a ghost myth at Ketebreka, which had been for a century. Every evening, during this week, the ghost would come strolling in the dormitory, visiting the bedside of the "homos". Every "homo" is expected to be in bed at lights out, at ten thirty p.m. with eyes tightly shut or asleep before eleven p.m. The story goes that the Ketebreka ghost would leave only if it is appeased with items of provision, especially; sardine, gari and "Joebed" black pepper (chilli sauce), which is referred to in the West African sub region as the "students companion". If the mythical ghost were not offered an appeasement each night that it visits, the one who does not place the offering on her pillow would be punished. She would be made blind and remain blind for the whole term. Gossip would circulate in town about the "homo who had become blind because she had failed to appease the Ketebreka ghost."

Chimbo enumerated a fictitious list of names of "homos" who were made blind by the Ketebreka ghost because they did not leave a conciliatory contribution on their pillows when it came to visit. The whole class was overcome with horror. She advised us, though, that we did not need to place all of our provisions on our pillows at once; just a few items each night would suffice.

We could not eat all the provisions in one night, I am sure, chimbo would be thinking because she paused for a minute.

INSPIRATION

The mythical ghost of Ketebreka was, in fact, the final year class. They would clad themselves completely in their white bed sheets, from head to toe and adorn dark goggles. They would collect the provisions from the "homos" pillows, spread a feast in the night in the house prefect's single room, enjoy themselves and leave the remnants about in the dormitory for the juniors to sweep the next morning The "homos" would think the ghost had accepted their appeasement offering.

Homo Naa Tomi was the youngest of four children. The three elder sisters had been students of Ketebreka. They had explained to Naa Tomi the fictitious story of the myth of Ketebreka. But had warned her that if she let the cat out of the bag and the seniors got to know about it, she would be punished.

Naa Tomi kept quiet about the story being made up and about a plot she had hatched with her sisters. Her senior sisters had prepared for Naa Tomi two different qualities of the black pepper; one was extremely hot containing extra quantities of cloves, the other portion was the normal fairly mild black pepper containing a lot of smoked prawns and smoked fish. Naa Tomi was to put the bottle with the extra hot black pepper on her pillow. She added gari, corned beef and two sardines on her pillow before she retired to bed.

The "mythical ghost" kept her promise to visit the first night. It was a Thursday night. All the final year students of Okropong House met in the house prefect's room to enjoy the inaugural feast. The house prefect had his own single room. Although they expressed their opinion of the chilli being unusually hot, it was so well prepared that they munched and enjoyed the feast. They described how very nice the food was, making human efforts not to laugh aloud to waken the juniors. Chimbo described the food as being luscious, another said appetizing yet another said scrumptious then yummy then delectable and finally mouth-watering. It had turned out to be a challenge for adjectives to describe the feast. The house prefect summed it all as tasty.

At about two o'clock in the morning, there was a trek by the seniors to the toilet. Chimbo was the first to complain of severe tummy ache as she had ploughed through the feast most enthusiastically. Their stomach had started to run and quite badly. One of them had grown so weak from the outpour that he thought their condition was no worse than the symptoms of cholera they had been told about at the hygiene class. Someone had suggested they should call the housemaster now as it was getting to be a matter of life and death.

Naa Tomi, aware of what would happen, kept her eyes half open watching the seniors as they trudge to the nature's room. She overheard one senior say to the other that her anus was burning as if a hot iron rod had been inserted there.

Naa Tomi smothered her laugh with her pillow.

Okropong House was short of toilet rolls the next morning.

Ama was fascinated by the eloquence of Aba.

"I am the eldest of four children; two teenage twin brothers and a baby sister," Aba said. "My brothers are very handsome and my baby sister is gorgeous. I am the least beautiful but I have my qualities too."

Ama was throbbing with anxiety to know more about the twins.

"Your twin brothers, are they identical? And what school do they attend?" Ama asked.

"Yes, they are identical. Surprisingly, only my mum can tell one from the other. I mix up their names, but our dad is worse. He never calls one by his real name. The boys are used to it so whatever name he calls they respond. Both are in their first year in Ketebreka boys' boarding high school. My baby sister is in her fifth grade. They are all doing well." Aba concluded.

"You are also beautiful, Aba. "Beauty is in the eyes of the beholder," as the expression goes.

"Unfortunately, I am the only child, but I have many cousins." Ama added.

"I attended Ketebreka girls boarding high school. And I was the captain of the school hockey team." Aba stated

Ama was very impressed with Aba since Ama knew Ketebreka high school has been consistently one of the top high schools in the country. They also won the inter-schools' hockey championship on several occasions.

"I attended Oboboshibie co-educational high school," Ama started to tell Aba about herself.

"Uuh! " Aba exclaimed. So you have boys in your school?" Did any of the boys fancy you?"

"You rascal, nobody did, or better, I did not look." Ama said light-heartedly. We did not play hockey in Oboboshibie but athletics was compulsory," Ama interrupted.

"Unlike you, I did not win any laurels in sports though I did fairly well in long jump and high jump and participated in the girls' relay event.

"Hei! High jump; I bet the boys will be admiring the "cute butt" when you were flying in the air."

"You are very sarcastic, Aba," Ama giggled.

The conversation switched on to the ordeal they had led themselves into—the medical education. They discussed the stories regarding how difficult the course is and how busy they were going to be. They encouraged each other to do their best as they locked in embrace.

Ama uttered in a soft voice, "we will carry through."

"I am starving. Is it time for breakfast yet?" Ama asked. Aba glanced at her watch. "Eight-twenty a.m. If we are quick we should just make it."

On their way to the cafeteria, they heard two fellow students discussing their doubts about how they would cope in human anatomy lectures.

"I heard that last year's students had to dissect cadavers," one of them said. Apparently a few of them collapsed out of sheer fright. One of the cadavers turned out to be a late uncle of one of the students."

It wasn't a surprise that Ama, eavesdropping on the conversation unexpectedly, did not feel at all interested in having breakfast. At the breakfast table, her sudden loss of appetite was evident to Aba. Ama just sat there, staring transfixed, at her bowl of cereals.

"Ama, that conversation seems to have troubled you. I have handled many dead bodies recently and I am okay. I know you will be, too. You just get used to it once you overcome the initial shock."

Ama turned her head slowly and now focused on her friend.

"What on earth do you mean by handling dead bodies? Are you a gravedigger or something?" Ama wondered.

"My parents are undertakers, and I sometimes helped them with the business," Aba continued. "Do you know my interest in reading medicine stems from working with the dead bodies? I will specialize in pathology when I qualify as a doctor."

Ama smiled politely turning her attention to the soggy mess in front of her that was her cereal.

INSPIRATION

A minute later Ama turned to Aba and enquired, " suppose during the rotations you found another discipline more interesting than pathology, would you change your mind?" Aba smiled and replied, " certainly not: my mind is made up."

"I would have thought it would be better for us to keep our minds open till after we have graduated," Ama advised. " Nevertheless you are entitled to your opinion," Ama concluded.

CHAPTER FIVE
Love is Blind

Girls," Kojo uttered, "I think we will have to hurry if we want to make it to the cafeteria for dinner. It is almost six p.m."

Ama winged, "I have an assignment to finish before tomorrow's lectures. I think I might give dinner a miss"

"What assignment?" Kojo enquired. "Can I be of any assistance?"

"No thanks. I'll be fine. Don't let me keep you. The canteen closes in about ten minutes. I just want to get on with this assignment and maybe check on some anatomy topics before tomorrow's lectures."

Ama thought, *does he not get the hint?*

"I shall leave you to it then. See you later on in the evening."

"Finally!" Ama thought aloud as Kojo left." There's being nice and then there's getting a bit overbearing." She turned her attention to the work in front of her.

Later on that evening Aba paid Ama a visit. "Ama, I think Kojo has a crush on you. His body language when he is around is so obviously screaming love. He talks endlessly about you in your absence. He obviously cannot survive a day without you being the focus of his attention or every third word in his vocabulary."

Ama interrupted, "Stop being silly, Aba. We hardly know each other. Anyway he is just being nice. That's all. You're mistaking that for something else."

"Nice, did you say? Is that the new term for it, then? Well, I cannot wait for a handsome man like Kojo to come along and be 'nice' to me." Aba teased. "From the look of things you have been preoccupied with his niceties. I am sure that book was on page 14 when we left you to go for dinner."

Ama smiled coyly recollecting the words of wisdom from Papa Addo before she left for the medical school.

"With freedom comes great responsibility and with responsibility comes temptation."

She gathered her books and excused herself. She needed a break from all this fuss so she decided to go to the library. She hoped the atmosphere there would drive her to study.

After a fruitless search for the international edition of the Anatomy and Physiology book written by Thibodaux and Patton, Ama approached the librarian for assistance. The "friendly librarian," as the students popularly called her, pointed out where she could find the book. Ama thanked her and left to look for it. Rumor had it this librarian was a former medical student who had dropped out suddenly because of an affair with one of the professors. Later on the professor had jilted her for her mate. The affair led to her breaking down psychologically. The students' library was said to be her only solace, the closest she ever got to the profession.

Ama read for another hour and finally decided it was time to return to the hostel. Her eyes were heavy with sleep. She headed straight to bed. At about twelve minutes past nine, she heard a knock on her door.

"Not again," she mumbled. "Can't I get some peace and quiet?"

She woke up reluctantly and enquired who it was. The voice that replied sounded familiar.

"It's me Kojo. I was just checking to see how you were getting on with the assignment. I brought you some food from the cafeteria."

Checking on me? Ama thought.

Due to her sleepiness she heard only bits of what Kojo was saying.

"Hold on a second," she said with some urgency as she put on something more decent. She quickly reached for her dressing gown, brushed her hair, powdered her nose and freshened her breath with antiseptic mouthwash. She then made for the door. She slowly turned the knob of her door to reveal that all-familiar figure.

"Oh hello Kojo," she muttered as she poked her head through the door opening. "I was tired when I returned from the library, so I went straight to bed. What time is it now?"

"It's twenty minutes past nine," Kojo answered. "Sorry, have I interrupted your sleep? I brought you some food from the cafeteria. Anyway I'll just leave it with you and allow you to get some rest." The tone of Kojo's voice showed that he really wanted Ama to allow him to stay awhile.

Ama flushed with embarrassment. It was as if Kojo had read her mind, as if she had thought aloud again that he was becoming a bit of a pest. It may have been just loud, enough for him to hear. Then again she was really too tired to care. She took the food and closed the door to the disappointment of Kojo.

As she got into bed, the phone rang. She tried to ignore it but the sound drove her insane. She finally answered, as the noise was not aiding her sleep. If only her alarm clock was as efficient at waking her up for those early morning lectures as this persistent ringing of the phone!

"Hello Ama!" It was Mama Addo. The tired body and heavy eyelids that were previously captive to the power of sleep had a new lease of life.

Ama answered, "Hello mama, how lovely to hear your voice again. How are Papa and everyone back home?"

"Everyone is fine. Grandma and Papa send you their regards.

The conversation soon focused on Kojo.

Mama Addo asked, "Do you know Mr. Alpomah's son? Mr. Alpomah is your father's friend."

"Which friend's son are you talking about?" Ama enquired.

"His name is Kojo. He is from Ganor village and he is also reading medicine," mama Addo answered.

"I now realize the person you are talking about," Ama recollected

We did not know he was in the university and reading medicine too until three days ago. His father called to inform us that his son had phoned them to tell them that he had met you and that you were getting to know each other." Mama Addo added.

"Oh did he?" Ama said searchingly

"We will talk some more when I come to visit you. It is late. Go and have some sleep. Good night," Mama Addo ended the conversation.

Ama went back to bed. It was now barely ten o'clock. Her mind kept wandering like a confused cockroach. Sleep had eluded her.

The telephone rang again. She took it asking herself who again this might be.

"Hello Ama, are you asleep?" Aba enquired with a touch of excitement in her voice.

"Not yet Aba," Ama replied. I am counting the ceiling rafts as the old folks would say. I am now unable to sleep after a couple of disturbances

"My roommate, Smillia has brought it to my attention that the second year girls have decided to form a netball team. You know the boys already have a soccer team. Smillia has asked me to canvas for more ladies in our class who would be interested to play netball. Your name and Patricia's immediately came into my thoughts. Think how the Wimba boys would be "spying" your "wicked" butt, as you dribble past their girls, with their degenerate butts. As a matter of fact I have already succeeded in enlisting the services of four of our classmates," Aba paused hoping for a response from Ama.

"You know Wednesdays are officially half days," Aba picked up where she had paused. "Lectures finish at one p.m. and we are free to do what we like. We could play netball just as the boys play soccer every Wednesday afternoon, with religious conviction. They formed a soccer team as a result and arranged the yearly matches with Wimba six years ago." Aba was speaking as Ama butt in.

"Oh! I read the notice on the board that our boys' soccer team would be going to play Wimba in four weeks time."

"You've got it, girl, that is the whole idea; to form a netball team and go with the boys to play the Wimba girls netball team," Aba quickly added, trying very hard to persuade Ama to join.

Aba succeeded in winning over Ama though Ama expressed reservation, as she had not played netball before.

"Don't worry, the first years could train separately to grasp the rudiments of the game before joining the second years.

Patricia has played netball seriously in high school and she belonged to a local netball club. She could help us with the fundamentals of the game," Aba suggested.

The few training sessions under the leadership of Patricia went well. They decided to join their seniors, feeling a lot more confident.

The second years now had a coach. The University sports coach had seen the second years playing and she was deeply impressed, as the university had a policy to promote sports on the campus. The coach volunteered to train them. They agreed and the coach had been coaching the second years for the past few weeks.

The appointed day for the joint game with the second years came.

At the first joint training session, the coach observed that Adzo, though very good at netball, was not making passes that appeared the obvious moves to make and which she was making predictably previously. She figured that Adzo was not passing to the first years. The coach, for that reason, beckoned to Adzo to come for a word. On seeing Adzo approaching the coach, Aba started to gravitate towards the pair and overheard the admonishing. Aba giggled. Adzo did not take the wrapping over the knuckles well and she stormed off the netball court.

Upset, the coach turned to Aba and wondered why Adzo had angrily left the court. By this time a few of the team members, including Ama, had joined Aba and the coach. Aba told the coach that it had been her impression since the first day of term that Adzo did not like to socialize with first year students.

Ama iterated, "It is her problem. Let's get on with it."

They played as though nothing had happened.

On the day of the match, the medic teams and their

supporters had an early breakfast. They were allocated two brand new medical school coaches. The two teams rode together on one bus and the supporters union went in the second bus. It was an enjoyable sixty-two mile journey to Wimba. Adzo was not on the bus. They sang, chanted and clapped all the way to Wimba.

The soccer and netball matches were played late in the morning, even though not simultaneously. The boys' soccer match ended in a pulsating two all drawn game. The girls, nevertheless, had a walloping defeat. The score was twenty-eight points to five. It could have been worse.

After the matches, the medic party was invited to lunch. They were treated to their favorite dish known by both students and, in fact, all students of the West African sub-region as "red, red". The medics enjoyed this treat of fried ripe plantain and sumptuous black-eyed bean stew made with quality "zomi" palm oil.

On the way back, the boys sarcastically praised the girls for work well done. One of the girls said they probably would have done better had Adzo been in the team. There was a loud ironic cheer. The soccer captain raised his voice and said, "It is the taking part, not the winning, as the Olympic ideals are." This was greeted with a cacophony of cries.

"In spite of everything, we exercised our hearts and other parts of our bodies. It is only a game after all," one of the girls whined.

They went back to their singing; chanting and clapping all the way back home.

Kojo was a handsome twenty-two year old young adult when he entered medical school. He was of average height and asthenic build. His close friends, in high school, knew Kojo as the handsome boy with one eye for women. He really enjoyed the company of girls and he did not toil much to win the heart of a lassie. That was why Kojo was so taken aback at the difficulty he was experiencing with Ama. His personality was the quiet but intelligent variety. He always obtained the top mark in his class. Kojo's physique portrayed direct contradiction of the pig-head tenacity of will in him. If one saw Kojo walking down the Apian Way, one would not think that Kojo was capable of killing a fly.

Kojo had absolutely no interest in contact sports. He however played the forty-piece African draught. The draughtboard has one hundred two-centimeter squares in two alternate colors, usually black and white. Kojo brought one draughtboard to the medical school and left it in the "Junior Common Room" for anybody interested to play. He soon gathered a group of enthusiasts and they organized tournaments amongst themselves. Although Kojo did not like contact sports he forced himself on to the supporters union bus for Wimba because both Ama and Aba were in the netball team.

It was no surprise, therefore, that a couple of pretty, light-skinned "alomos" occupied Kojo's attention for the whole period of the matches. "Alomo" was the term given to a gorgeous lady by the lads. Kojo scarcely saw a single move of the netball match, not even when Aba and Ama were on court. As for the football he appeared not to understand what was happening. It was amazing that in a country so fanatical about soccer somebody would be so ignorant about the game.

Kojo had an uncle, Lawyer Alpomah, who lived in the city with his wife, Auntie Clara and their only daughter, Geraldine, who was five years old. Lawyer Alpomah owned a very successful legal firm in the city. Kojo had three brothers and two sisters. Geraldine had nobody to play with so Lawyer Alpomah asked His brother to allow Kojo to come and stay with his family in the city. Mr. And Mrs. Alpomah agreed. At the age of six Kojo transferred to the city. It had been the wish of Lawyer and Mrs. Alpomah to have a son of their own but had so far not been successful.

Kojo and Geraldine grew up together, attending the same schools. In their teens Geraldine played cupid for Kojo with the many daughters of her uncle's influential friends. Kojo showed special interest in Christabel. Geraldine secretly hoped that the relationship between Kojo and Christabel would mature into a permanent bond. Geraldine, Christabel and Kojo scored very good grades at the matriculation exams qualifying them for university. Geraldine and Christabel were however sent to university abroad to read law.

Kojo visited Ganor village sparingly, often for a few days during his holidays. Lawyer Alpomah, time and again, convinced Kojo's brothers and sisters to come over and spend the holidays with them in the city.

They enjoyed their vacation.

Kojo had skeletons in the closet, which nobody in the medical school knew about. There was a gossip in some quarters of the city that when Kojo was in his final year at high school, he frequented the village nearby to buy beans and gari with zomi palm oil. It was not so much the beans and gari that Kojo was interested in though the food was very appetizing. It was the figure behind the stall selling the food; a young, pretty face, wide-eyed, nineteen-year-old lassie he was interested in. Kojo salivated whenever he got there not because of the food but because he fancied the girl. Maybe that was why he enjoyed the food so much. He tried to catch the attention of Dedo and found the response inviting. Kojo became certain that there was chemistry there. He decided to test the waters. One Saturday evening during entertainment he absconded. He went to purchase the usual. Unfortunately Dedo was not behind the stall that evening. Dedo's mother was behind the stall. Kojo fibbed that he forgot to collect his change from Dedo when he bought food the other day. He had come for his change. Dedo's mum asked Abeshi to go and get the change for Kojo. Kojo took his chance. He followed Abeshi to the house, which was only a short distance away. Abeshi knew about their flirtation so she left as soon as she called Dedo that Kojo wanted to see her. Dedo was shilly-shally. Kojo saw Dedo's hesitation. He stepped forward and gave her a peck on the lips. She smiled invitingly.

"Won't you invite me in?" Kojo asked.

Kojo did not wait for a reply. He held Dedo's hand and invited himself in. Things progressed fast as if choreographed. Within a short time there had been a ten-minute of beastly activity, a rumpy-bumpy, on the sofa in the lounge as there was nobody in the house. Kojo was expressing his physical passion.

Dedo gave a jerk and collapsed. She did not respond to call and shaking. Kojo panicked. He dressed quickly and ran outside intending to escape. Fortunately a taxicab was passing by. Kojo frantically waved at it to stop. He told the driver that his sister had collapsed in the house but their parents were out. The two sent her to the hospital.

Dedo was known in the casualty department as a cardiac patient. The cardiologist quickly saw her and she ended up on the theatre table for a triple by-pass.

She made uneventful recovery.

Kojo returned to school as soon as Dedo was admitted. When Dedo's family returned home, Dedo was nowhere to be found. The mother knew she had complained of feeling unwell. Aware of her cardiac condition, she rushed to the hospital and learnt of the emergency heart operation. Dedo's mother thought some good Samaritans saw her predicament and sent her to the hospital. She said a quiet blessing for the good Samaritans.

Back in school, Kojo's closest friend, Tete, found that Kojo was very worried and nervous. He asked where he had been to and what was wrong? Kojo took him aside and devoured to Tete all that had happened.

"Ei Kojo, you must have a wicked prick," Tete teased

Kojo became furious. The next day after the compulsory morning service Kojo went home to tell his uncle what had happened.

Seeing how disturbed Kojo was Lawyer Alpomah decided not to be hard on Kojo. However, he cautioned Kojo.

Lawyer Alpomah drove straight to Ganor village to inform Papa Alpomah the exploits of his son.

Lawyer Alpomah succeeded in sweeping the matter under the carpet.

CHAPTER SIX
If at First You Don't Succeed

W hen shall we go out Ama," Kojo enquired. "It seems we have been working non-stop since we arrived on campus. We need to socialize too. As the adage goes,

All work and no play make Ruben a dull hippopotamus."

Ama turned and gave Kojo a look of astonishment.

"Makes Jack a dull boy, " she replied.

"I thought you were not paying attention," Kojo said cheekily. "Would you like to go to the cinema with me tonight? There is nice roman...I mean a nice film on at the Orion in town."

"I don't know. I'll think about it and let you know. I think I might be busy then. Why did you invite me in particular? I am sure there are other female students around besides me who would like to go."

That in my book is referred to as a low blow statement, Kojo thought very disappointedly.

There was an understandable awkward silence after that comment by Ama. Kojo wished the ground would open up and swallow him alive. The silence seemed to go on for eternity. For Kojo it did. Ama was reveling in the moment. Kojo stood there mummified wondering for a moment whether Ama had suddenly changed or whether she was just playing hard to get

"Again she uttered, "I shall think about it and call you.""

Kojo left feeling downhearted. It overshadowed the rest of his day. The sharp rejection lingered over him like a dark cloud. Still he thought to himself that he could win her over. It was just a matter of time.

He obviously does not know when to give up. One has to give the man some credit though. The guys got guts, Ama thought.

For some reason or other Ama now felt quite bad that she had turned down Kojo's invitation. After all, it was just a bit of fun. Kojo was a good-looking guy. Many girls would die to go out with him.

What in god's name, am I playing at? She thought. Hang on! I am just as beautiful as the other girls are but I also do not desire to appear too keen. I must not lose sight of my purpose here, to qualify as a doctor.

Kojo was still upset when he got to his room. He paced up and down for a while when a thought came to him.

Should I invite Aba?

He picked up the phone and dialed Aba's number.

"Hello Aba it's Kojo. There is a nice film showing at the Orion. I was wondering if you'd want to come along. My treat."

"I beg your pardon?" said Aba.

Here we go again, thought Kojo.

"Yes Aba, you heard me right. Will you accompany me to the Orion this evening?"

"Sorry, Kojo, I am busy this evening. Why don't you invite Ama? I'm sure she'd love to go."

"I did, but she was too busy. Some excuse about doing her hair or something."

"Really? Well, if the truth were to be told I don't feel like a movie tonight, either. Thank you for the phone call, though."

As soon as Aba hung up she called Ama. "Hello, Ama! Are you busy?"

"No," Ama muttered. "Why do you ask?"

"I am coming over for a chat." Aba hung up the phone before Ama could get another word in.

Aba changed into a casual clothe and hurried to Ama's room.

"Ama, Kojo just called me. He sounded a bit despondent when he spoke to me on the phone. He phoned to invite me to a movie but I turned him down. Why would you not go with him? I suggest you rethink his invitation. It would do both of you some good to go out. You need a break from all the study, and he...."

Ama interrupted, "I think it is too late now. I have already told him I am not certain whether I will go to the cinema and he understood. Anyway he asked you as well, didn't he?"

"But you could still change your mind. You've got sufficient time to get ready for the movie," replied Aba.

The phone rang as the two friends progressed to a different line of conversation. Ama answered the call. "Hello, Kojo."

Aba got up to leave when she heard who the caller was.

Two's company and three is a crowd, Aba recollected an old local saying.

Kojo arrived on time to pick up Ama outside her residence. She had definitely made an effort for the night. She had to after her earlier attempts at playing hard to get. She wore a figure hugging dress and her hair was in a ponytail. Her appearance was simple but elegant.

Kojo's eyes slowly traced the contours of her body. He couldn't be more pleased with what he was seeing. He felt like a kid in a candy shop.

"Tu regarde aveuglant," Kojo said in the most sensuously provocative voice he could muster.

"I didn't know you spoke Spanish," Ama exclaimed jokingly.

That sounded French to me, Kojo retorted cunningly.

Kojo escorted her to the vehicle he had hired for the night. Ama's eyes lit up at the sight of it.

He speaks French and has a nice car as well, she thought.

Kojo and Ama sat in the car.

"To the Orion cinema please," Kojo instructed the driver.

"Ok," replied the driver and he turned on the music.

Kojo immediately turned to Ama with a deep feeling of satisfaction and commented,

"This is Slim Busta featuring Kanto West, the latest music on the urban scene. I love it."

Ama smiled.

" I have not heard this music. Do you mean some music is played only in the city?"

The driver overheard their conversation and joined in.

The driver, in fact is privy to this plot. He is Kojo's new friend who drives a breath-taking Lexus car.

The driver added, " Slim Bosta is a nice, clever, sensitive, and the most generous man I have ever seen. I met him on the pediatric ward the other day when I was visiting my sick daughter. He was doing charity work; presenting loads of gifts to the kiddies."

He dropped them off at the Orion.

Kojo had purchased the tickets in advance.

"Theatre four please, enjoy the movie," the attendant said, after inspecting the tickets and tearing off the counterfoil.

Kojo and Ama entered theatre four and chose the seats at the far end of the back row. Ama was pleasantly impressed at the façade of the cinema and the beauty of the interior decoration. That was Ama's first ever visit into a modern cinema house. Filled with excitement, Ama gave Kojo a peck on his right cheek.

The movie was a classic tale of love, deceit and revenge... During a scene of passionate kissing, Kojo placed his right arm on Ama's shoulder. Ama did not object.

Another scenery showed a heavy love entanglement in a gorgeous hotel. The couple in the film had danced to a mouth-watering, newly released "hi-life" music. The wiggling of the lady's waist to the tune of the music drew a lengthy laughter amongst the audience. Kojo laughed more heartily. He used the laughter to get a little closer so that the arm Kojo had over Ama's shoulder slipped under Ama's arm to her breast, and Kojo pressed Ama against his side. Ama smiled

When the end credits finally rolled up it greeted with ovation and cries of "Encore."

From the Orion the two proceeded to the south central district for a meal. It was a three-course meal, in a small but authentic Chinese restaurant. Kojo had definitely done his research beforehand.

During the main course, the conversation turned to the movie.

Ama retorted, "I think Mariah was wrong to lead Rolando on and reject him."

"I agree," Kojo replied." She was manipulative and cunning. Mariah did in the end pay the price, though. It was kind of ironic that she ended up with Rolando."

"Yes, who would have predicted that?" continued Ama, smiling her seductive two-dimple smile.

Kojo dropped Ama off and even managed to sneak in a cheeky kiss. There was buoyancy in his stride as he walked towards the waiting car. Kojo climbed into the back of the car and sat back with a proprietary air unusual for him. Kojo was bent on enjoying, to the full, the "presidential privilege" his good friend was according him. The friend drove off. Ama returned to her apartment still buzzing from the night. That night her pillows got one heck of a beating.

CHAPTER SEVEN
One Step Forward, Two Steps Back

Her first year was very hectic. She adapted well to her new conditions and progressed steadily with lectures and assignments.

Ward 4 was extremely busy. Ama and her fellow medical students were on their morning rounds with Professor Lamprey. Like her colleagues, Ama was beginning ward duty today. The entire first year had been spent learning the theory. The second year was designed to give them hands-on health care experience. The atmosphere was electric with excitement. The ward rounds lasted for one hour and at the end professor Lamprey expressed satisfaction at their debut performance. Ama was to present her patient's case history at the next ward round.

Ama later returned to interview her patient, one Mrs. Tobilus.

Mrs. Tobilus is a wealthy philanthropist, who has given a lot of money and her time to the community. She has also donated much expensive equipment to the University Teaching Hospital; the latest donation was an MRI Scanner.

Mrs. Tobilus protested strongly to Ama that since her admission all she did was answer doctors' questions. She said if the doctors spent as much time and energy in actually remedying her situation as on their constant inquisition she would be fully recovered and discharged by now.

"I am tired and frustrated with you doctors for continuously subjecting me to a barrage of questions. What is this, the Spanish inquisition or a hospital? I thought you were trained to know why we are sick. Stop with the questioning because none of you have given me any answers yet." Mrs. Tobilus snapped at Ama.

Ama realized that her patient was not in the mood to tolerate any form of dialogue, be it on a professional level or otherwise. She just listened attentively, nodding and gesturing occasionally in acknowledgement of her patient's distress and concern.

Ama left Mrs. Tobilus feeling rather dejected and upset. The ward manager, Sister Kudzo, noticed that Ama was looking depressed. She called Ama to her office and told her that she was not looking herself that morning. She asked to know why. Ama recounted her experience with Mrs. Tobilus. She was upset because she was to present the case history to Dr. Lamprey at the next ward round. She was finding difficulty getting Mrs. Tobilus to co-operate with her.

The ward sister reassured Ama that patients are sometimes difficult and we the staff need to exercise patience and tact to persuade them. When patients are not in good mood it is always difficult to communicate with them. Sister Kudzo agreed with Ama that Mrs. Tobilus was probably not in a good mood that morning. She promised to talk to Mrs. Tobilus herself.

She came back with a message for Ama that Mrs. Tobilus would speak to her the next day.

Ama felt relieved.

Ama arrived on Ward 4 very early the following morning.

Picking up Mrs. Tobilus's folder, she approached her bedside wearing a smile on her face.

"Hello Mrs. Tobilus, how are you doing this morning? Did you sleep well last night? What about breakfast, did you enjoy it?"

"Yes," she responded. "I could not complain."

I may be able to get through to her today, Ama thought. Just keep the communication going and keep away from anything too medical. That should break the ice.

The ploy certainly worked as they talked for about half an hour. Ama took down the relevant notes and finished off the rest of her rounds.

The anatomy lectures went on for two hours longer than expected.

At the end of lectures, Kojo approached Ama.

"I have not been seeing much of you these days."

"Yeah I know. I have been busy on the ward."

"Are you enjoying the ward experience, then?"

"Brilliant," she answered. "What about you Kojo, how are your male patients doing? Is Aba enjoying the experience on the male urology ward as well?"

" I cannot advocate for her, but from what I see she is totally enjoying it," Kojo said amusingly, adding," but for me as long as they would be cooped up on their beds 24/7."

Most of the patients on the male urology ward are old and frail.

"You do not sound too cheerful. What is wrong?"

"I am just tired from the physical and emotional strain of ward duty that's all. I did not realize just how energy sapping it could be."

"How did lectures go today? I saw you catching a few naps during today's lecture, or were you just resting your eyes?" Ama said jokingly.

"Yes, I enjoyed today's lecture. You know it's my favorite, but I felt tired at the end," Kojo replied, trying to force a smile that looked as weary as his entire body did.

Kojo's lack of enthusiasm for chatting did not seem to dent Ama's willingness to carry on the conversation. "I spoke to mama and papa yesterday and they asked me to extend their love to you."

"Okay," Kojo mumbled. Fatigue had reduced him to managing just one-word answers. Ama continued, "they asked how we were coping with the new term, which brings me on to my next request. I need your help with Anatomy. Can you meet me at the library this evening? I did not understand some of the points raised in today's lectures."

"Yes I will be there myself so I will catch up with you then."

"Thank you," Ama said as she approached Kojo and kissed him lightly on the cheek.

As Ama had guessed Kojo did not turn up at the library. At about 9:30p.m. Ama phoned Kojo to come down to dinner. He had just woken up and sounded a bit groggy. "What's the special occasion?" Kojo asked.

"There is nothing special. I just thought I'd cook us something nice."

"I am on my way". He arrived with a bottle of palm wine.

"This is for you, to say sorry for not being able to turn up at the library. I must have overslept."

"It is okay. Thanks." Ama beckoned Kojo in.

What an opportunity. This is a good time to show her that I love her, Kojo thought. Maybe get past the kiss on the cheek. He was ecstatic. This was the closest he had ever gotten to her except for the time he sat next to her at the pharmacology lecture.

During the meal, Kojo and Ama exchanged romantic glances.

The communication was easy going and the drinks went down well with the meal. He helped her with the washing up. During this time Kojo's mind wandered as he fantasized about how firm her breasts really were underneath all that clothing, and how curvaceous her derriere really was. This was eating him up from the inside.

"Shall we listen to some folk music?" Kojo asked. They sat next to each other listening and humming. As the night wore on they became increasingly relaxed.

Soon Kojo and Ama were in the center of the room dancing to the music. "I hope it will be my turn to cook you a meal next time around, if you will allow me, of course." Kojo whispered.

The hairs on the back of her neck stood up as she felt his warm breath tingle past her ears. Ama responded almost breathlessly.

"No, I love to cook for the men in my life."

"The men in your life?" Kojo enquired looking into Ama's eyes.

"I see only one man standing here."

Ama smiled her lips now moistened with excitement. She had never felt a man's body this close before and she loved every moment. "I love to cook for the man in my life," she repeated.

As soon as Kojo heard this he knew that this was his moment. He moved in and took Ama's lips on his, tenderly kissing her. Their bodies pressed and soon they were not moving to the beat of the music but to their hot, steamy passion.

Kojo's hands began to explore her body, feeling her through her clothes. She did have a plump derriere, so soft to touch.

He caressed it as their kissing became passionate. He felt her response to his touch and that gave him more uncontrollable desire.

Ama sensed she was now not in control of her body let alone the situation she was finding herself in. She was moist with excitement, her legs beginning to feel like jelly, her nipples hard and sensitive. She trembled with Kojo's every touch, particularly when he caressed her derriere aggressively. Sooner or later she knew he would take her.

Kojo began slowly lifting her dress up towards her hips. Ama could now feel the cool breeze of the night flowing between her thighs. At that moment she suddenly pushed Kojo away and drew her skirt back down.

"We are just good friends and nothing more, okay? I think we are getting a bit carried away with this. Please leave."

Kojo couldn't believe what he was hearing. That statement was enough to make any man permanently impotent. Kojo stepped back in amazement. He adjusted himself and headed straight for the door.

"Thanks for the dinner," he said as he exited.

Kojo soliloquized as he made his way to his flat. He kept asking himself:

Kojo what have I done wrong?

He bumped into one of the senior students. He asked Kojo what was wrong as Kojo was obviously talking to the air.

"I was recollecting the words of a song I loved so much, Satchmo's Shadrack Mezzac and Abednigo. I learnt it in school. I have only just heard it played on the radio," Kojo replied.

"Okay, see you."

Kojo continued towards his flat.

Kojo suddenly stopped, turned and traced his footsteps back to Ama's door. He knocked, announcing his presence.

"Ama it is me, can you let me in? I want to talk to you."

Ama reluctantly opened the door. Kojo stepped inside the room and left the door half closed. He stood near the door. He apologized to Ama.

"I am sorry for stepping beyond my boundary. I do not know what came over me. Please forgive me."

"If I lead you on then I also apologize to you," Ama said, refusing to accept that she may have lead Kojo on.

"I have nursed a soft spot for you since I met you and I want to let you know that."

"Kojo thanks for telling me this, but you know we are here to study. I think we should put our whole mind to it. We could just be friends. That should be enough."

After accepting each other's apology, Kojo left, afraid to offer his hand for a handshake.

CHAPTER EIGHT
A Love Lost

Ama woke up very late the following morning. She hastily dressed and rushed down to Ward 4.

"Late night?" asked Ward Manager Kudzo as Ama entered Ward 4.

That was the last thing Ama wanted to hear from the Nursing Sister in charge of Ward 4, also called Ward Manager.

"Where is Mrs. Tobilus, Sister? I did not see her when I passed her bedside."

The Ward Sister explained to her that, Dr Lartey, the senior registrar on duty, had referred her for a chest x-ray. Mrs. Tobilus had been complaining of cough and associated chest pains.

Ama was still talking to the Ward Sister when she saw Mrs. Tobilus returning from x-ray.

"Good morning, nice of you to join us bed-ridden patients. Can I have a word?"

Ama answered, "Of course you can. That is why we are here. I will be with you in a minute."

Ama finished her conversation with Ward Sister Kudzo and began reading through Mrs. Tobilus' folder. Ama went to Mrs. Tobilus' bedside.

"I suppose you have been told that I was sent for a chest x-ray this morning." Mrs. Tobilus said. "I have been experiencing chest pains for the past week that became quite unbearable last night. I had wanted to tell you but I thought,

Why bother her? She is just a student doctor.

"You don't look your usual cheery self today."

"I had a rough night. Anyway it's you we're worried about not my sleeping patterns," Ama responded. You should have told me of the chest pains. Even if I was not able to help I could have taken notes and informed my superiors."

Ward 4 duties were a blessing in disguise for Ama that day as they took her mind off the events of the previous night.

Kojo did not make his usual evening visits for a while. Neither did Aba, Ama realized. Ama could understand Kojo but not Aba. It was as if Aba was avoiding her. Maybe Aba did not want to get caught in the middle of the situation between her and Kojo.

That weekend Ama decided to pay Aba a visit. Unfortunately, Aba was not in. Aba's roommate informed her that she had gone out with a mystery man that afternoon. Ama thought that was probably why Aba had been avoiding her.

The following morning Ama received mail from home announcing the demise of her grandmother. She was quite heart broken and promptly phoned home to extend her condolences to her parents.

"I am really sorry to hear of Grand's death Mama I wish I could come down to help but I am really busy with clinical practice."

"Do not worry, my daughter. Everything is organized and we shall give Grandma a fitting burial. Take good care of your self."

Just as Mama Addo was about to hang up, she quickly passed on a message to Ama that she had almost forgotten?

"I nearly forgot to tell you that Kojo's parents visited to offer their condolences. How are you two getting on?"

"We are fine. However, we do not see each other much these days since we are both busy working in different wards. When is Grandma's funeral?" Ama enquired.

"I have already told you that, dear. It is next Monday," her mum replied. "You don't seem to be concentrating on what I am saying. Are you sure all's well with you?"

"Be strong, Mama, and extend my greetings to Papa. I have to go now. There is someone at the door." Ama knew she had fibbed but the conversation was getting a bit tricky. She didn't want to discuss the whole Kojo experience. She instinctively headed to Aba's room to inform her of her Grandma's demise and, she hoped, to get some comfort. She could do with a shoulder to cry on. She momentarily wished Kojo were around to offer her that shoulder.

On the way to Aba's room, Ama bumped into Smillia, Aba's roommate. "Is Aba in?" she asked. Smillia nodded as she hurried past. What Smillia had failed to say was that Aba had company of the male persuasion and that was why she had to leave the room.

Ama was so anxious to chat with Aba that she didn't even bother knocking once she got to Aba's room. She opened the door and burst in.

"Aba, you won't believe what has happened to me this week. First of all." Ama stopped dead once she saw who else was in the room with Aba.

"Kojo! What are you doing here? Aba, what are you doing with Kojo?"

Kojo and Aba were sprawled on the bed in a rather compromising position. In fact, Kojo had his hands half way up her skirt.

Ama was transfixed to the spot when she walked in on Kojo and Aba.

A sort of paralysis had spread over her limbs while an intense pressure was mounting in her chest

"So this is why you two have been ignoring me! I could understand you Kojo, but Aba, why! Has he told you what happened between us? Well, aren't either of you going to say something?"

"I was just comforting him, Ama. He told me what happened between you two, so I was giving him a shoulder to cry on."

"It looked to me when I walked in like you were about to give him more than a shoulder to cry on, Aba. I can't believe you could do this to me."

"Look here, Ama, I am giving him a soft shoulder to cry on. Some shoulders are too hard to cry on, you know." Aba said angrily.

Kojo joined the heated exchange. "Look, Ama, it's your loss. You fobbed me off so what's the problem? We can choose to see who we want"

"Kojo is right. We have not done anything wrong. It is your loss. I told you I wouldn't mind a hunk like him being 'nice' to me. You had your chance and blew it!"

Ama was seething, but deep within her she knew they were both right to an extent. The sight of Kojo's hands still in the position she caught them in nauseated her. To think just over a week ago she was almost in the same position. She stormed out of the room and went outside for fresh air. She wasn't bothered where, as long as it was far away from Aba's room. As she walked, the words "look Ama, it's your loss," rang through her head.

When Ama got back to her room, Adzo had returned from the library. She was in the kitchen preparing cocoa drink. As Adzo picked up the kettle to pour the hot water into the mug, Adzo heard the door slam. That startled her a bit and Adzo scalded herself. She went to find out who had banged the door. She saw Ama sitting on her bed, holding her head in her hands.

"Are you okay?" Adzo enquired.

On hearing Adzo ask the question, strong emotions welled inside her: she began to sob.

Ama found difficulty expressing herself clearly as she tried to speak. Her sobs reached crescendo.

Adzo barely made out Ama was trying to say. She went back into the kitchen and returned with the mug of chocolate drink and offered it to Ama.

Ama took the drink though hesitatingly.

Adzo went back to the kitchen to prepare herself another cup of cocoa drink. As soon she left, Ama placed her mug of cocoa drink on the bedside table, her eyes rooted to the steam arising from the cocoa drink. The sobbing had pitted down considerably.

"Why don't you take a sip of the beverage, Ama? You will feel better if you do," Adzo recommended.

"I know we have not interacted well but the adage in our part of the world commands that one should not continue to hold a grudge against another when the fellow is bereaved, or taken ill or has just had a baby. There is automatic or spontaneous truce. What I am trying to say is that I am all ears if you want to share your feelings."

There was a brief moment of silence.

"A little over a year ago, I was in the same state as you appear to be today. My twin sister was involved in a fatal road accident. We were identical twins. Our dad had picked her from the evening drama lesson. He sustained serious injuries but luckily he survived. I was heartbroken when I heard of the tragedy. What made matters worse was that I could not attend the funeral. I was in the middle of my exams. My roommate and other friends gave me their unqualified support, to which I have been grateful even to this day," Adzo said.

Whilst Adzo was speaking, Ama picked the beverage and took a sip.

"I had a call from home that my dear grandmother had died,"

"Oh, sorry to hear that," Adzo said.

There was another brief moment of reticence. An air of calmness had replaced the previous charged atmosphere.

"You know our traditional belief that when our dear ones die they are taken by the spirits of our forefathers to where their ancestors are. Your granny is in good hands. Hence you must not worry," Adzo consoled Ama.

For the first time since the two have been roommates, they had a meaningful chat and even hugged each other.

CHAPTER NINE
Joseph

On the way into the lecture hall Ama approached Kojo. Since the altercation they had drifted apart.

"Kojo, could you spare me a minute?" Ama asked. "I need to talk to you."

"I have an appointment to see Professor Lamprey after lectures. I am free to chat with you after that," he replied.

"How things change! It wasn't so long ago that Kojo would have given the world to be in my company. Now he does not even notice me. I am an insignificant nothing," Ama stood there for a while thinking.

Ama couldn't concentrate much during the lectures as her attention drifted towards the figure sitting in the second row below her. At the end of the lecture Ama seized the opportunity to quickly talk to Kojo He was walking out of the lecture room chatting with Ablah.

Ama approached.

"Hello, Ablah. Did you find today's lectures interesting? Oh, hello, Kojo. I didn't realize you also knew Ablah."

Kojo just excused himself and left the two to carry on with their conversation.

"Yeah, I enjoyed the lecture very much. Moreover I have a patient with a similar condition in the ward and so the lectures made me understand the condition better," Ablah replied.

"Really, so how did the patient make you understand the condition?" Ama was keen to know.

"No. I have a patient with the same condition," Ablah stressed recognizing that Ama wasn't taking any notice of what she had been saying. Kojo seemed to be in a hurry all of a sudden.

"He was in the middle of telling me something. I think he wanted some feminine advice on how to treat his new girlfriend on her birthday. I think you might know her, Ama? Anyway I have to rush off as well. I have invited a few first year interns for dinner."

They went their separate ways.

Soon after the meeting with Professor Lamprey, Kojo rang Ama.

"I am free to have that chat you were asking for earlier today. Shall I come over or would you like to come here?"

"No, not right now. I have to see my patient on the ward. I promised her yesterday I would see her after visiting time is over. I need to go now. I shall call as soon as I come back."

When Ama arrived on the ward, she approached Mrs. Tobilus' bedside.

"Hello, Ama. Thanks for coming. Let us go to the patients' lounge for a bit of privacy to talk."

Ama helped her out of bed and they walked towards the lounge.

They talked for a while without really centering on a specific topic

Ama was wondering all the while why she had been invited. At first she thought it was something medical. Well, so she thought, until Mrs. Tobilus let slip:

"I am very impressed with you. I admire your approach to work and your manners are highly praiseworthy. What I am driving at is whether you would like to meet my son. Possibly go out on a date with him. He is more than happy to meet you.

He will be picking me up tomorrow when I get discharged. I'm sure you will be on ward duty. I have requested that you sort out my discharge."

Ama was slightly perturbed by the line the conversation was taking. She mustered up courage and told Mrs. Tobilus that the arrangement with her son was not acceptable.

"Thank you for having me in your thoughts. I am sure your son is a lovely man." Ama felt she had to say something that wasn't too harsh on Mrs. Tobilus, who appeared excited and thought she could play cupid for her son.

Rightly or wrongly, Ama did not think it was right to be that emotionally involved with a patient or her closest relative. Thus, Ama decided to play safe.

Ama left the ward and returned to her room. After gathering her thoughts she phoned Kojo to see if he was still available to chat. Aba picked up the phone. In the background Ama could hear somebody chatting. The voice sounded that of a male. Ama thought the voice might be that of Kojo's. Ama decided against going to see Kojo that night and after a slight pause hung up the phone without saying a word.

Ama was on duty the next morning in charge of "discharge planning". She was on edge that day because she realized she would most likely meet Mrs. Tobilus's son. She was attending to Mrs. Tobilus when two male figures entered the ward and approached the bed.

"That's my son and his friend coming," Mrs. Tobilus said. Ama looked up and for a second thought she could make out who one of the men was. Her intuition was confirmed when they arrived at the bed.

"This is my son and this is his friend Kojo. Joseph arrived yesterday and stayed over at Kojo's place last night," Mrs. Tobilus said.

"You must be Ama, My mum speaks highly of you. Thanks

for taking care of her whilst she has been here. I thought I'd get you a little something to show our appreciation."

Joseph handed her an envelope and a bunch of flowers. It was practice not to accept gifts from patients, but Ama felt compelled to break the rule on this occasion.

"Is she ready to be discharged then?" He asked.

"Yes," Ama replied. " The doctors came on rounds yesterday and decided that your mum was well enough to go home."

"Oh how rude of me, I didn't introduce you to my friend, Kojo. This is Ama, the best doctor on Ward 4 according to my mum. I am yet to find out how good she really is," Joseph said as he gave Ama a cheeky look.

Politely, Kojo shook Ama's hand and they both played along as if they were meeting for the first time.

"Is it me or is there some tension in the air? The way you two shook each others hands, one would have thought you had a past," Joseph observed, obviously not realizing they actually did have a past.

Ama was glad when she finalized all her duties on Ward 4 that day. She normally looked forward to clinical practice but today was a rare occasion of

"Get it over and done with as quickly as possible and disappear."

Admittedly, Ama's first impression of Joseph was good. She found him to be handsome, tall, hunky and soft-spoken. The decorations in Mrs. Tobilus's single room on Ward 4 bore witness to how wealthy Joseph's family was. The bouquet of flowers Joseph gave Ama was stunning. The choice of colors and the arrangement were immaculate.

She returned to her room exhausted. The significance of

the day's activities wandered in Ama's mind as she strolled home after work. As she threw her bag on the bed the envelope fell out onto the floor. She picked it up and opened it.

Unfortunately, Ama did not reflect seeking advice from anybody regarding the issue as to whether a doctor, and for that matter a medical student, was allowed to date her patient or the patient's son. She did not even consider whether that oversight could be a mistake. She could not think of herself bringing this topic up with any of her friends.

For the first time Papa Addo's advice did not creep into Ama's mind.

She stripped and entered the shower and gave herself a good "soaking".

Whilst in the shower, Ama's mind went haywire, thinking about her meeting with Joseph.

Am I quietly beginning to fancy Joseph? Or did the short period of promenade home from the ward arouse my emotions. Should I get on with it, come what may? After all who will not date a wealthy woman's son?

Ama recollected Aba's statement,

"I cannot wait for a handsome man like Kojo to come along and be nice to me."

Should I wait tot be told again:

"Ama it is your loss................"

Ama finished taking the shower, still consumed in her thoughts.

On her way out of the bathroom, Ama suddenly noticed the envelope on the floor. She picked it up and opened it. . She hadn't been that excited about opening an envelope since the day she received her medical school sponsorship letter a few years ago. When she opened the envelope, it emitted a wonderful scent. Within the envelope was a beautifully handcrafted card with a note, which simply read

"Thank you. Joseph."

Joseph had also coyly left his mobile number along with the note. It was just legible beneath his signature. Ama didn't notice it at first and put the card on her bedside shelf. She proceeded to dress up.

Whilst she was dressing up, her next-door neighbor popped in.

"Take a seat Patricia. I have just had a shower and I am dressing up. I will be with you in a minute. There's a cold drink in the fridge. Please help yourself."

Patricia poured herself some fruit juice and sat on Ama's bed. She noticed the card and picked it up inquisitively to find out who had sent this lovely card. She couldn't help being nosy, especially as the scent from the card was quite enticing.

"Ama, who's Joseph?" she probed as she read the card.

"And what is he thanking you for?" Patricia asked excitedly

Ama joined Patricia in the bedroom. Ama wore a traditional multicolored tie and dye "kaba" blouse with a matching wrap skirt and she was drying her hair. Ama sat on the bed. Patricia immediately got up and took over the drying of Ama's hair.

"What hair-style would you like?" Patricia asked.

"I don't know," Ama answered.

"Let me plait it and decorate it with beads for you whilst you tell me about this mystery card- sender. I have some nice, expensive beads in my room." Patricia suggested.

"No, I would rather love a weave into "corn roll," Ama requested.

"Ok. You will need to sit on the stool." Patricia advised.

Ama sat on the stool in front of the dressing mirror and Patricia started to weave Ama's hair.

"Joseph is a son of one of my patients. I was taking care of his mum. It's just a thank you card. Nothing more, nothing less," Ama broke the silence

"That's a strange way to spell thank you. 024834.... They look more like numbers to me. 0 for what and what does the 4 stand for and an eight too this is funny 8. Is it a coded message?" Patricia asked.

"Where did you get those numbers from, Ama?" Patricia asked.

"So are you going to call the number?" Patricia probed further.

Ama just ignored Patricia's continuous questioning. Patricia sensed that Ama had become uncomfortable with her non-stop probing so Patricia switched the topic to course work, until they finished the hair styling.

They, however, spent the rest of the evening chatting, particularly about Kojo and Joseph. Ama couldn't avoid the subject as Patricia had a way of gleaning information from Ama.

Patricia left Ama's room at eleven p.m. Before Ama went to bed she took one last look at the card almost memorizing the hardly legible cell phone number, which she had not previously noticed.

CHAPTER TEN
All Night Long

It was about three weeks before Ama finally called the number on Joseph's card. Joseph was surprised when he got the call. He was not surprised at who it was on the other side of the line, but in how long Ama had taken to call him.

"You took your time, Ama. I know the writing was almost illegible but I didn't realize it would take that long to decipher."

Ama laughed softly at that statement. That was all the encouragement Joseph needed as he began working his charm with words. Joseph had a way with words and certainly with the women in his life. Ama was no exception.

The conversation ebbed and flowed nicely. The more they spoke the more Ama felt drawn to Joseph. Amidst the chitchat and flirtatious banter, she even managed to ask about Mrs. Tobilus. Joseph certainly impressed Ama. Mrs. Tobilus did have a point when she spoke so highly of him. He was her only son so that was to be expected, but Ama was starting to agree with her train of thought.

By the end of the call Joseph had Ama eating out of the palm of his hand. He had managed to arrange a date with Ama for the following weekend. Maybe Ama was now opening up to the opposite sex. Maybe she just gave into Joseph's persistence. Whatever the case she had unknowingly taken the first step towards a strange twist of fate. It's funny how a single decision can change ones destiny.

Ama was buzzing all week as she counted down the days to the date with Joseph. She got her hair styled and her nails painted. You name it. Pedicure, manicure, this girl left no stone unturned in her quest to look drop-dead gorgeous for the date.

When the day arrived she did look extremely dazzling. One could light the room with her smile, and the scent she wore made her seem almost edible.

Joseph was true to his word. He picked her up on time and gave her a night to remember.

Joseph treated Ama to a series of whirlwind dates. One week it was an outdoor cinema, the next a walk in the park, then there was the meal in the seafood restaurant. Joseph made her feel special and she never thought about Kojo or any of her friends, as a matter of fact.

What Ama failed to realize was that her fondness for Joseph made her detract from her close friends. All her conversations were centered on Joseph, and after a while her friends grew weary of her. They'd visit and she would ignore them as soon as Joseph called. It was Joseph this, Joseph that.

Ama's girlfriends thought Joseph was nice but they smelled a rat. It was a shame Joseph's expensive cologne masked that when it came to Ama.

Aba had the audacity, as Ama put it, to question her judgment. That was an eventful day at the canteen. The moment Aba mentioned the subject the atmosphere became heated, expletives were exchanged and Aba was escorted out of the canteen sporting a head full of rice and mutton stew.

Now you can understand how Ama drove away her friends. One by one, they left her company. Rumors began circulating and with them a different picture of Ama.

Ama, however, was not bothered by all the fuss as long as she had Joseph. He told her she was beautiful and intelligent. He made her feel special. "You don't need them," he would say. "They are just jealous because you have come from humble beginnings and are dating a wealthy hunk of a man."

"Yes you are a hunk of a man and not just a hunk, but my wealthy hunk of a man," she would reply.

Now I'm no relationship expert, Ama thought. When a guy with Joseph's reputation gives as much as he has done, there should come a time when he would expect some sort of payback. Is it what I have heard somebody refer to as "sods law"? Come on the man not only thinks he's an Adonis, he has the bravado to say so, and so he says whether people want to hear it or not!

It was the evening of August 4 when it happened. Joseph was about to cash in on his investment. He invited Ama over to his house one night for another one of their regular dates. They had a habit now of eating at Joseph's every Friday night. Mrs. Tobilus had suggested a family meal once so she could have Joseph and Ama around. They had just continued with the tradition though now Mrs. Tobilus wasn't a part of the event. She knew when she wasn't wanted. After all these were young lovers enjoying their time together? She had been at that stage of life so she understood the little hints she got at the dinner table anytime they had their Friday get- together.

Anyway, back to the story.

It was the evening of August 4 when it happened. Joseph had invited Ama over for dinner. After much thought he settled on rice and black-eyed beans stew. His mother was away with an aunt for the weekend and he therefore had the house to himself.

Ama made her usual effort to look exquisite. On this occasion she wore a ruffled skirt and top with a low, plunging neckline. The stiletto heels she had on made her hips move with wonderful grace. Joseph had a glint in his eye when he let her in that night. As she entered and walked towards the living room, he stared hungrily at her hips. He licked his lips.

They sat for a while, watching music videos and chatting merrily. Joseph had the habit of being flirtatious and throwing in erotic comments now and again about Ama. She was used to that and loved the attention. That evening however there was something different about the tone he used when throwing in those random comments.

They settled at the table to eat, but after a few forkfuls Joseph suggested they took their plates into the living room to relax and eat on the sofa while watching the music videos. Halfway through the meal Joseph left for the kitchen to get some drinks.

"What would you like to drink with the meal?" he asked. "Normally red wine goes well with it but I know you don't particularly like the taste of it so I have got some fruit juices here for you."

That's sweet, Ama thought.

"I will have some of the wine, don't worry. I am just not used to it that's why I tend not to drink it. I suppose it's an acquired taste."

Joseph brought a bottle of red wine and returned to the kitchen to get some glasses. For someone who said wine was an acquired taste, Ama acquired it quickly. She was soon sipping her fifth glass, Joseph tacitly encouraging her on.

As the night drew on, the more glasses of wine she drank the more incoherent she became. Joseph took Ama's plate from her and took it to the kitchen as Ama could hardly stand up from the sofa.

When Joseph returned Ama was lying spread-eagled on her back. Her eyes were glazed over and her ruffled skirt was halfway up over her thighs.

Joseph stood over Ama for a while allowing his eyes to meander her forlorn body drinking in the mind-boggling spectacle lying below his tall figure. Ama tried to reach up to him. Joseph instinctively thought Ama wanted him to help her sit up on the sofa. However, when Joseph felt her soft, warm hands his heart pounded and he moved closer to Ama. He longed for her. He debated whether to stop for a moment but something deep inside urged him on. Why should he miss such an opportunity?

He was so close he could smell her and feel her hot breath on his face. He moved his nose over her face then towards her neck and drew in deep breaths as he took in her scent.

Suddenly he was totally overcome with lust. Before he could realize what he was doing he was licking the side of Ama's face slowly then towards her lips where he kissed them softly. Ama responded and partially opened her eyes, seeing only a blurry figure and image in front of her.

At that point Joseph's kisses became more intense, bordering on the painful. Ama's weak body struggled to break free but that juxtaposition proved difficult to breach. The atmosphere was charged and Joseph's senses were heightened. The ticking clock on the living room wall sounded like explosions. It was nearing midnight. He tried lifting her skirt further up but Ama managed to put up some resistance. That was met with rage as he shoved her ruffled skirt and slid her underwear to one side partially ripping it in reply. Like a flash of lightning he worked his way up her thighs.

Ama felt a sharp pain in both sides of the inner thigh as Joseph attempted to part her thighs with his knuckles.

Ama's resistance, which was initially feeble, suddenly gained momentum. What Joseph had not appreciated was that his judgment, regarding his prowess, had been drastically clouded. Joseph secretly gulped large quantities of rum and champagne each time he went into the kitchen alone.

Joseph was now getting tired. He became aware that Ama was persistent with the resistance so he attempted to calm her down in his usual soft, but now stuttering voice.

"Darling," Joseph said. " I am just expressing emotional love and physical passion."

Both appeared to have passed out with exhaustion.

When Ama woke up, it was six o'clock the next morning. Fortunately, it was Saturday and Ama was off-duty. Joseph was still deep in sleep.

Ama quickly reached for her bag and sneaked out of the house.

She hailed a taxi home.

When Ama got back to the flat, Adzo was still in bed. She tiptoed into the bathroom and had a quick shower. She put on her makeup and hid her torn knickers in her drawer and locked it up, hoping to discard it later. She sat on her bed and started to sob quietly. Ama's sobbing aroused Adzo. Adzo sat up. She noticed Ama was in distress mode. She enquired,

"What is wrong, Ama? What again? You don't look alive this morning? Is there another bereavement? I brought home curry takeaway yesterday evening and waited for you all night but you did not come home. Where did you go?"

"I went out with a friend," Ama answered in a low tone. "He hurt me emotionally."

"What!" Adzo yelled. "What may have happened if I may ask?" Adzo pried scanning Ama's eyes. Ama stared into Adzo's eyes with a copula expression. Adzo knew Ama was having difficulty divulging what the matter was. Hence, she got up and left to have a quick shower. Adzo boiled the kettle and prepared tea, which the two drank together.

"Go to bed Ama and have a sound sleep. We shall talk further after I return from work," she encouraged Ama. She left for work.

Ama took a couple of sips of the tea Adzo had prepared for her and went to bed.

She could not sleep. She turned and tossed in bed having horrible daydreams. Eventually she snatched twenty minutes of slumber, which to Ama felt a century. She woke up, sat in her bed and struggled in her mind what to do next. She arrived at nothing. So she decided to carry on with it and hope the bad issue resolves itself.

She made an impulsive decision to go to the library hoping if she were able to concentrate, her mind would be taken off the incident.

She gathered her books and left for the library.

CHAPTER ELEVEN
Repercussions

The following few days were difficult for Ama as she withdrew into a shell. She had already lost the confidence of the few friends she had when she went through the "Joseph" period. She needed someone to talk to, as her ordeal played on her mind like a broken record.

At lectures it was obvious she lacked focus. In some instances she got to lectures late or missed them altogether. Even when her mama phoned she couldn't mention the situation as she thought of the shame that would bring to the family and what her folks would think of her. For all she knew they would think that city living had turned her away from the values she was brought up with.

Ama was a mere spectator of her life now. The longer she went without seeking some sort of help, support or solace the worse her psychological state became. The girl who didn't drink alcohol now began to find comfort in drink. Strangely enough it was in wine.

On the third week after another night in with a few bottles of wine Ama decided to pay Kojo a visit. The alcohol had given her a bit of courage, or so she thought. In reality she was now bordering on desperation.

She stumbled over to Kojo's block. She stood outside his door for a while, thoughts running through her mind. As she was about to knock on the door Aba opened it. Ama's momentum carried her into the room. She stumbled towards a chair and sat down.

"Where's Kojo?" she asked. "I need to speak to him

"Kojo isn't here. He has gone to buy some dinner for the two of us. We are eating take away tonight like we always do on Wednesdays. Go and come back another time," Aba replied.

That wasn't the sort of welcome Ama was expecting.

"I said I want to speak to Kojo," she continued muttering under her breath.

"What is wrong with you Ama? You spurned the man's advances. What do you want with him, especially at this time of the night? And what is that smell? Have you been drinking?"

"He raped me," Ama began saying repeatedly under breath. "He raped me." "Jos—." Before Ama could continue Kojo entered the room.

"What's going on here," he asked. "Ama?"

"She keeps muttering stuff under her breath. I think she mentioned rape." At that statement Kojo instantly dropped the takeaway he had purchased.

"Rape!!" "Who? When? How? What are you on about Aba?"

Ama was an absolute mess at this stage. She sat coiled up in the seat, rocking back and forth. She started sobbing and tears rolled down her cheeks. With each tear came forth a release of deep-seated pain.

"Aba, make her some hot, sweet chocolate drink please," Kojo asked.

"What? I am not leaving you a second alone with her. She is probably lying. She has always been jealous of us and now she's trying everything she can to break us up."

Kojo lost his temper for a brief moment and screamed back.

"I said make her some chocolate. Just do it! Please."

As Aba left for the kitchen Kojo moved closer to Ama. Rubbing the tears off her cheeks, he asked her softly what happened.

"He raped me...Joseph," came the reply.

Kojo was taken aback. "When did this happen?" he asked. Ama recoiled into her shell and fell silent. At that moment Aba entered the room with the hot chocolate and an unwelcoming scowl on her face. She hadn't seen eye to eye with Ama ever since their argument in the dining hall.

"Put the chocolate drink down next to her," Kojo beckoned.

"Well, what's she mumbling now?" Aba asked.

As Kojo was in the middle of answering Aba's cell phone rang. She picked up the call and walked back to the kitchen. Ama began mumbling Joseph's name again. One could almost sense the fear in her voice.

"What!" Aba screamed from the kitchen. She immediately ran into the room and attacked Ama, whose body was now lifeless. "You liar. You liar!" she repeated angrily.

Kojo pulled her off of Ama.

"What are you doing? Can't you see she is unwell? She's been raped by"

"Joseph," Aba finished.

"She claims she's been raped by Joseph. Ungrateful bitch! She wasn't saying that when he was spending all that money on her. He stops spoiling her because she's getting a bit pompous and she claims now that he has raped her. All her friends have been complaining about her newfound character. She's from the village, gets a taste of the high life and it gets to her head. Why don't you take your rape story back to your village?" Aba whined.

"Look at you sitting there, a true picture of a drenched chicken," Aba said to Ama insultingly.

This infuriated Ama. Ama sprang up from her seat, as if possessed by the spirits of the gods of the village, wagging her right index finger at Aba.

"You are the liar!" Ama accused Aba. You have been spreading nasty rumor that Dr. Landey, the orthopedic consultant, has had sexual relationship with me. What a load of nonsense."

Before Aba could put in a word, Ama grabbed Aba by her hair and pulled her on to the floor dragging her.

Kojo, helplessly, tried to separate them. He could not get Ama to release her hold.

Screams and cries drew a small crowd of neighbors to the scene.

They succeeded in separating Ama and Aba. The small crowd left.

Kojo did not know what to do next. After a short period Kojo asked Ama if she would like him to accompany her to her room? On hearing this suggestion from Kojo Aba stormed out of the room.

Ama ignored Kojo's request and left. Kojo, rather concerned about Ama's mental state, followed Ama to her door.

Kojo bid her goodnight and left.

CHAPTER TWELVE
Dark Hour

Ama's claims about being raped started to put a strain on Kojo's relationship with Aba. Aba became obsessed with the notion of Ama's ploy to ruin her relationship with Kojo and went on a personal vendetta to discredit Ama. She began spreading vicious rumors throughout campus.

Ama never really took any notice of the gossip and coldness that was shown towards her. She had enough to occupy her mind. She had summoned the courage to get some tests done for any sexually transmitted diseases. Ama was told that the results would be ready five days from the day of the test.

Ama did not want the report to be delivered to Ward 4 so she arranged to collect it personally from the laboratory on Friday afternoon.

After lectures, on the appointed day, Ama set off to collect the results. When she stepped out, it was unusually dark. The sky was covered with ceaselessly active dark clouds, except at the far horizon where a strip of lightness prevailed. Ama instantly recollected her geography lessons and the word "cumulus" clouds came to her. She chuckled because she remembered her classmates nicknamed their geography mistress "cumulus". Ama's classmates would count how many times the geography mistress mentioned the word "cumulus" during geography lecture. Long streaks of lightning split the clouds furiously and impatiently only to melt away instantly. Then the heavens opened. When it began, the rain fell like large pebbles. Ama's face had a good thrashing by the hailstones.

The laboratory was a fair distance from the medical school, where the lecture theatres were.

Ama took refuge at a bus stop

Fortunately, Kojo was driving past and stopped to pick her up. At first she was reluctant to accept the ride, but Kojo convinced her. He also went out of his way to take her to the laboratory.

Kojo had compassion for Ama. Indeed Kojo had a soft spot in his heart for Ama. (This is Aba's apprehension.) The journey seemed to Ama to go on for an eternity. Kojo tried to make conversation but Ama really wasn't interested. Kojo wanted to ask why she was heading for the hospital, though; he figured it must be something associated with Ama's rape.

The rain was heavy that afternoon and although Kojo had the windshield wipers on full throttle visibility was still impaired. The fact that some of the streetlights had failed didn't help matters either because most of the oncoming cars had their headlights on full beam. This further impaired his visibility of the road. The only sensible thing for Kojo to do was to drive at a safe speed so he could take a longer time trying to make out the road ahead.

They were a few minutes from the junction that led into the main hospital when Ama coughed a little. Now, considering the fact that she hadn't made a sound since she climbed into the car, this slight cough caught Kojo's attention. He instinctively turned to see why Ama had made that noise. Maybe he thought she was finally trying to make conversation.

"Pardon?" he asked as he turned his head to face Ama.

"Watch out!" came the reply.

When Kojo instinctively turned his head he had steered off the road into the path of an oncoming vehicle. He swerved. But it was too late. He crashed head-on into the approaching vehicle. There were extensive damages to both cars and serious injuries to Kojo and Ama. The only passenger in the other car, fortunately, sustained minor abrasions and lacerations.

Staff at the accident and emergency department, near-by, heard the large bang and rushed to the scene. They quickly assessed the injured and transferred them to the emergency suite. The Emergency Suite was very busy when Kojo and Ama were taken in. They were wheeled in on separate trolleys. The specialist staff started monitoring them immediately.

"Blood Pressure fifty systolic, Pulse barely palpable," the attending staff announced. The "Shock Protocol" was immediately set in motion; the patient needed resuscitation and urgent blood transfusion to replace the severe blood loss.

This patient is male, aged mid twenties, and has sustained serious frontal lobe head injuries, and acute blood loss. Time was of the essence with regards to this patient. To the untrained eye, the scene seemed chaotic, but to the Accident and Emergency staff, everything was under control. This was just another normal day for them.

"This patient needs immediate surgery. Take him straight to theatre room 7. I will get scrubbed. Somebody beep Dr. Sagoo, the consultant anesthetist, now and get him to Theatre Room 7," the neurosurgeon on duty ordered.

Emergency blood for transfusion arrived from the Blood Bank. The patient's blood belonged to the blood group "O" Rhesus Positive. This blood was compatible with the patient's blood and could therefore be transfused into him.

The transfusion started immediately and the blood pressure and pulse steadily improved. He was transferred to

Theatre Room 7. Dr. Sagoo was already in Theatre Room 7 with his assistant, Dr. Abede. Before the patient was placed on the operating table, one of the third year medical students, called Agodo, entered the theatre. He recognized the patient as Kojo and he immediately fainted. Dr. Abede attended to Agodo whilst Dr. Sagoo proceeded to anaesthetize Kojo.

Dr. Sagoo announced that Kojo was anesthetically ready for the operation. Dr. Kapra, the neurosurgeon started to operate. His aim was not only to save Kojo's life but also to give him the best chance of having a better quality of life post surgery. Dr. Kapra taught the medical students and the junior doctors the complications that could occur from the injury, the surgery, and the long road of recovery ahead for Kojo.

They admired Kojo's courage as he fought to free himself from the embrace of the grim reaper.

Ama was also taken into the Emergency Suite. She was quickly assessed. She was breathing normally and the Blood Pressure was ninety systolic and forty diastolic (90/40 mm. Hg) and the pulse was one hundred beats per minute. Her general condition was not as bad as Kojo's and was therefore placed on strict "observation" just in case she was bleeding internally. Routine bloods were taken for tests and a drip set up to keep the vein open should she require transfusion later. The intern advised Ama to donate urine for further tests. Ama obliged. Though not routine the doctor ran a quick pregnancy test on the urine specimen. He had recollected an advice given to his class during a lecture in gynecology a few years ago at medical school.

"Any woman, in the childbearing age, who comes to consult you whatever the symptoms, should be considered also to be pregnant unless proved otherwise and if she complains of repeated fainting attacks, ectopic pregnancy must be considered, until proved otherwise,"

This working advice was thought appropriate by the lecturer because the complications of illegal (or "backstreet") abortions and ectopic pregnancies had been, for a long time, among the leading causes of death amongst young women especially teenagers and students in the country.

Ama's urine test came back positive for pregnancy. The intern informed his superior, who wrote a referral for "gynae" opinion and faxed to the gynecology consultant on duty. The gynecologist came immediately to review Ama. He ran a scan and suggested that Ama was pregnant He ordered a re-scan in two weeks to confirm how old the pregnancy was.

"Would somebody find out who she is and contact her parents, guardians, anybody who knows her." Shouted the Charge Nurse. The Emergency Team retrieved their possessions from the crash scene, and left them with the hospital social worker. She had already begun efforts to contact both casualties' guardians.

It wasn't until late the next morning that both Kojo's and Ama's parents were told of the news. Both families took the news badly. They rushed to the hospital.

Kojo's parents were the first to arrive at the hospital. When they got there, they headed straight to the receptionist and began frantically demanding information about their son's health and location. The receptionist tried to calm them down so that she could understand their request since she could not make head or tail of what they were saying.

Kojo's parents managed to control their emotions.

"Our son, Michael Kojo Alpoma, was admitted here last night. We just got the message this morning. Where is he? What is happening?" asked Mrs. Alpoma, Kojo's mother.

As the scene continued Aba also entered the hospital and carried on to the reception desk.

"Hello, I'm here to see Michael Kojo Alpoma, please," she said.

On hearing that, Mrs. Alpoma turned her attention to Aba.

"Do you know my son? What happened to him?" she asked with an unevenness of tone

The receptionist did not like the inquisition and therefore interrupted.

"Please take a seat and let me get the Ward Manager. She will be able to help you." The receptionist beeped the Ward Manager to the reception area. When she arrived she took control of the situation and beckoned the three highly emotional people to her office. She then proceeded to beep the doctor in charge of Kojo's medical care to her office.

The doctor entered about twelve minutes later, followed promptly by Papa and Mama Addo. When he entered, Mr. and Mrs. Alpoma stood up from their seats anxious to hear what he had to say.

"Please take a seat," the doctor said as he also beckoned to Papa and Mama Addo. "We have brought you here because your son, Kojo, and your daughter, Ama, were both brought into A&E last night at approximately ten minutes to seven. They were both involved in a car collision. Kojo sustained a serious head injury and was sent straight away for emergency surgery. The surgery was successful and he is currently recovering satisfactorily."

Mr. and Mrs. Alpoma were listening attentively, however, they filtered the words and only took in what they wanted to hear. As soon as Mrs. Alpoma heard the words "currently recovering satisfactorily" and "surgery was successful," she breathed a sigh of relief and embraced her husband. The doctor continued,

"Nevertheless, Kojo sustained damage to the frontal lobe which may lead to slight complications in the future. When the wound heals it will leave scars on the brain, which might cause changes in Kojo's personality. He may also become forgetful at times and it is most likely he has suffered some short term memory loss."

Aba couldn't take what she was hearing very well and stepped outside midway through the doctor's discussion. Mr. and Mrs. Alpoma still held their embrace long after the doctor had finished his explanation. They just stood there, motionless, as if they had been caught in a time warp.

The doctor now began explaining Ama's prognosis.

"Ama was the more fortunate of the two victims. Although she had lost a lot of blood she was now in a stable condition. She sustained minor bruising, some lacerations and a broken bone in her arm," demonstrating on his arm the equivalent site of the fracture. "She is a very lucky lady. We also ran a scan on her and we think she may be pregnant."

The doctor was quite pleased to be giving some good news to, at least, one of the families. He smiled at Papa and Mama Addo. Papa Addo kept a straight face. They were shocked at the news of their daughter's "pregnancy". Mama Addo sprang up from her seat, as though a giant African scorpion had stung her, her mouth ajar. The expression on her face was a sight to behold.

"Sorry doctor, but I don't think you have got your diagnosis right. My daughter can't be pregnant. Pregnant? How, and with what, and by whom exactly? She is not married and she is certainly not the "Virgin Mary" so how can she be pregnant? I want a second opinion."

The doctor was astonished at how the Addos had taken

the news. He gave the Ward Manager a wry look and simply excused himself from the office

The two families were left to gather their thoughts in the Ward Manager's office.